THE
GOOD WAR

THE
GOOD WAR

TODD STRASSER

DELACORTE PRESS

Text copyright © 2021 by Todd Strasser
Jacket art copyright © 2021 by Phil Pascuzzo

All rights reserved. Published in the United States by Delacorte Press, an imprint of Random House Children's Books, a division of Penguin Random House LLC, New York.

Delacorte Press is a registered trademark and the colophon is a trademark of Penguin Random House LLC.

Visit us on the Web! rhcbooks.com

Educators and librarians, for a variety of teaching tools, visit us at RHTeachersLibrarians.com

Library of Congress Cataloging-in-Publication Data is available upon request.
ISBN 978-0-593-17365-7 (trade) — ISBN 978-0-593-30780-9 (lib. bdg.) — ISBN 978-0-593-17366-4 (ebook)

The text of this book is set in 11-point Electra LT Std.
Interior design by Jen Valero

Printed in the United States of America
10 9 8 7 6 5 4 3 2 1
First Edition

FOR BARB, LIA, GEOFF, JULIA, AND BEN

THE
GOOD WAR

PART ONE

WEEK ONE

The morning bell rang. Goofy Foot, aka Zach Cook, dodged through the mob funneling into Ironville Middle School. Wearing a backpack and carrying a skateboard, he weaved and sidestepped through the crowd. When he accidentally bumped into a girl with long black hair, she snapped, "Watch where you're going." Other kids gave him dirty looks as he squeezed past them. But they were the bad guys. In Goofy Foot's mind, he was in the video game called *The Good War*, and the entire school was enemy territory.

After stashing his skateboard in his locker, Goofy Foot enters the pissorium and is greeted by the harsh odor of bodily waste. He ducks into a stall for shelter before the next bell. Goofy Foot does not want to risk being ambushed at a urinal by the bad guys.

The boys' room door opened with a creak, accompanied by the voices of Gavin Morgenstern and Ratface Fugard. In the stall, Zach held his breath. Ratface, whose real name was Crosby, picked on Zach every chance he got. Zach knew that if Ratface caught him in the pissorium, he'd be dead meat.

Goofy Foot hunkers down inside the stall. Through the sliver between the stall door and doorstop, he spies on the enemy's activities.

"I heard Robbie's parents moved to Franklin so he can play on their football team," Ratface said, standing in front of the mirror and raking his fingers through his dark hair. His long nose reminded Zach of a rat.

"Yeah," Gavin said at a urinal.

"Wish my mom could do that," Ratface said. "It totally sucks that Ironville canceled football. Imagine if we could all move to Franklin and play?"

"It's a big school," said Gavin, who had red hair and freckles. "Think you could make the team?"

"Hey, I may not be big, but I'm fast," said Ratface.

Hidden in the stall, Zach wondered about that. Ratface might have been fast, but he was small. Smaller even than Zach. There were plenty of bigger kids who were just as fast. Gavin, on the other hand, was the biggest kid in the grade. He reminded Zach of Duke Nukem. You wouldn't think a kid that brawny could be quick and agile, but when they played flag football or basketball in gym, the team with Gavin on it always won.

Gavin backed away from the urinal. He cleared his throat loudly, then gazed up at the ceiling.

Inside the stall, Goofy Foot looks upward. His eyes take in an astounding sight. Stuck to the ceiling of the pissorium are a dozen dried brownish-green hanging loogies! Like a cave with mucus stalactites.

His head tilted back, Gavin hocked and fired. *Splat!* His

loogie smacked into the ceiling and stuck. But from the middle, it drooped, stretching like light brown Play-Doh Slime until the bulbous end broke and fell to the floor with a *plop!*

"Darn," Gavin grumbled.

"Maybe next time," Ratface said.

The bell rings, and Gavin and Ratface leave the bathroom. Once again alone, Goofy Foot exits the stall. But before he goes to class, he stands in the middle of the pissorium, face tilted upward. It is too tempting not to try. He hocks his own glob of slimy ammunition, aims, then fires!

Alas, his mucus projectile lacks firepower. It doesn't get halfway to the ceiling before it sputters and falls short.

It plummets back down and splatters all over Goofy Foot's face.

○

The bell was going to ring at any moment. Ms. B had finally managed to get Principal Summers down to the computer lab to show her the eight shiny new Providia gaming computers that had just arrived.

Principal Summers was a petite, neatly dressed woman with short black hair. She was also a tough, but always fair administrator. She slid a glossy red fingernail along the top edge of one of the twenty-four-inch monitors. "How can these not cost us anything?" she asked.

"We got them with a technology grant for low-income schools," Ms. B said. "It even includes an upgrade for our internet connection, new routers, and these gaming setups."

Principal Summers nodded slowly. Ms. B could tell that the principal had doubts about encouraging eSports at school. "Can we use them for anything besides gaming?" the principal asked.

"Absolutely," said Ms. B. "When they're not being used by the eSports club, they're available for schoolwork. And they can run three-D modeling programs and Photoshop, which our present computers can't handle."

Principal Summers picked up one of the new headsets that had come with the Providias. "I just don't see how an eSports club will ever replace the football team."

"It's awful that the school board had to cut football," Ms. B said, "but hopefully, this will give students something else to focus on and get excited about."

Principal Summers smiled thinly, as if she wasn't sure that was true. "Do me a favor? Make sure the rest of the staff knows that these computers came from a grant. I don't want anyone to think our school spent its meager funds on an eSports club."

Ms. B promised she would. She'd known from the get-go that getting behind eSports in school was risky. But without their football team, she felt they had to do whatever they could to encourage school spirit.

The bell rang. Principal Summers had to get back to the office for the morning announcements. Ms. B went to her classroom. Even though school had been in session for only a few weeks, she no longer had to check the seating chart to know who wasn't there. One student had been out for two days with a cold. Another's mother had emailed that morning that her son wasn't feeling well. And that left Zach Cook, who always came to class late.

Ms. B settled at her desk. She was eager to see how the kids would react to that morning's announcements.

○

Sitting in the front row in Ms. B's class, Caleb Arnett chewed anxiously on a pen. Just a short time ago, on the bus to school, he'd overheard Crosby telling Gavin about his plan to cheat on the geometry test that afternoon. Caleb didn't think of himself as an angel, but he hated when kids cheated. The way he saw it, if everyone were allowed to cheat in school, that would be fine. Because it would level the playing field. But most kids chose not to cheat. Not always because they believed it was wrong, but because they knew that if they got caught, it would be a stain on their reputations. Caleb might have only been in seventh grade, but he was smart enough to know that once you got labeled a cheater, it stuck forever.

Caleb was trying to decide what to do about Crosby when the classroom door swung open, and Zach dashed in late as usual, lugging his backpack and wiping his face with a paper towel.

"Why are you late this time, Zach?" Ms. B asked.

Zach was a squirmy kid who never looked you in the eye. Hardly spoke. Had more nervous habits than anyone Caleb had ever seen. Bit his nails, chewed on his lip, picked at his scalp, blinked excessively, couldn't sit still. "Sorry, Ms. B," Zach said. "I spit myself."

The class erupted into laughter. It was classic Zach Cook. Even as he'd said it, his eyes flicked for an instant toward the class to make sure they were listening.

Ms. B stiffened. "Zach!" she snapped. "What did you just say?"

"I said I *spit* myself." Zach repeated the word with emphasis.

The class was still tittering, but Ms. B relaxed. "Oh, I thought you said something else. Take your seat. And maybe tomorrow, by some miracle, you could be on time?"

Zach went to his desk at the back of the room. Caleb returned to wondering what he should do about Crosby's plan to cheat.

The class might have found Zach's antics funny, but to Emma Lopez they were deeply disturbing. Emma couldn't imagine drawing attention to herself like that. Just the thought of all those eyes on her made her want to slide down in her seat and disappear. If *she* ever made a spectacle of herself, what would they say about her? What if someone had their phone out and posted it to Snapchat? Think of the memes! The idea of being singled out online terrified her.

Just then the morning announcements began. "Heard about the new eSports club here at Ironville Middle School?" the student announcer asked. "What? Did you say *eSports*? You heard right. Thanks to Ms. B and Caleb Arnett, we just got eight brand-new fully loaded Providia X-Master gaming PCs. If you're a gamer, you'll want to hit the informational meeting in the computer lab after school today to learn more."

As usual, half the class wasn't listening, but Emma's ears perked up. *An eSports club?* She glanced at Caleb, who sat a few seats away. He was a tall, slender boy with light brown hair and ears that stuck out just a tad too much. At that moment, he was grinning with pride. As if feeling Emma's gaze, he turned and looked at her. Emma felt her face grow warm and hoped that it didn't look like she was blushing. She mouthed the word "Thanks" to him. Caleb's grin grew broad.

Meanwhile, those who had listened to the announcement started chatting with their neighbors. From a few rows away came Crosby's loud voice: "What's the point? We can play all the video games we want at home."

A reply came from an unexpected source: a new kid at school whose name was Nathan. "On a Providia X-Master? That's the fastest, most powerful gaming computer there is. It's what all the pros use."

Crosby raised his hand. "Ms. B, how fast are the processors?"

"What's the refresh rate of the screens?" asked Nathan.

"Do they come with gaming mice?"

"And those cool LED keyboards?"

"You'll have to come to the meeting to find out," Ms. B said, pleased to see that at least some of the students were interested. She rose from her desk. "All right, everyone. There's an assembly in the gym. Let's go."

The class lined up and filed out of the room. Ms. B started to follow. Being the last person to leave, she looked back to make sure the classroom was empty. It wasn't. Zach was still seated in the last row, staring intently at a notebook propped against the edge of his desk. He was so engrossed in whatever was in that notebook, he hadn't noticed that the rest of the class was gone.

"Zach?" Ms. B said from the doorway.

Zach raised his head and blinked in astonishment. Ms. B saw the sudden panic in his eyes as he looked around, no doubt wondering where everyone had gone.

"The assembly?" she reminded him.

Zach quickly slid the notebook into his backpack and headed toward the door.

"Just a minute," Ms. B said. "I'd like to see that notebook."

○

The hall was filled with kids walking toward the gym for the assembly. Gavin and Crosby were a few steps ahead of Caleb. Once again, Caleb thought about Crosby's plan to cheat on the geometry test. Every morning, Gavin and Crosby got on the bus a few stops after Caleb's. Two sixth graders usually sat behind Caleb, and Gavin and Crosby often sat behind them. The sixth graders were both awestruck and terrified by Gavin. They'd be jabbering like a couple of meerkats, but as soon as Crosby and Gavin sat, they'd shut up and listen. Crosby's voice carried, so even when he was talking low, Caleb could hear him. On the bus that morning, Crosby had told Gavin how he planned to cheat that day. Most of the time when Caleb heard about cheating, it involved a phone or a calculator, but Crosby's plan was so low-tech, it was almost brilliant.

What bothered Caleb was that unless he did something, Crosby would probably get away with it. Walking with the crowd toward the gym, Caleb looked around, expecting to see Ms. B, but she wasn't with the class. So this could be the perfect time to find her and tell her what Crosby planned to do. But Caleb would still have to return and sit with his class during the assembly. Then he noticed Emma walking behind him. She was a nice kid and one of the smartest in their grade. Sort of quiet, but during the announcement about the eSports Club, she was the only one in class who'd smiled and mouthed "Thanks" to him.

"Hey, Emma?" Caleb said.

Emma looked up at him with wide, startled eyes. "Yes?"

"I have to go back to class," Caleb said. "Save me a seat?"

Before Emma could answer, he turned away down the hall.

When Caleb got to the classroom, Ms. B was talking to Zach. In her hands was an open notebook. Caleb was surprised to see a phone nestled snuggly in a cutout space inside. It appeared that Zach had used an X-Acto knife to cut into the pages so he could hide his phone there.

When she saw Caleb, Ms. B closed the notebook. "Why aren't you at the assembly?" she asked.

"Uh, there's something I need to talk to you about," Caleb said.

Ms. B raised an eyebrow uncertainly. "Wait in the hall. I'll just be a minute."

She closed the door. While he waited in the hall, Caleb thought about Zach's phone-in-the-notebook scam. It was pretty clever for a kid who often walked through the halls with his hoodie pulled so tight that only his nose and one eye were visible. A kid who'd been pantsed practically every day in fifth grade and who some called Zach the Wack because of how weird he could be.

A few moments later the door opened, and Zach and Ms. B came out. "You'd better hurry," Ms. B said. Zach began to run down the hall toward the auditorium. "Zach!" Ms. B called. Zach skidded to a stop. Ms. B pointed up the hall. "It's in the gym."

Zach spun around and raced in that direction. Now Ms. B turned to Caleb.

"We're late," she said. "Let's walk and talk."

As they headed toward the gym, Caleb told her about Crosby's plan to cheat on the geometry test that afternoon.

"I already know about it," Ms. B said. "But thanks for telling me."

○

Ms. B was puzzled. So far this morning, two students had informed her that Crosby planned to cheat on that afternoon's geometry test. One of the sources had been Caleb, which did not surprise her. But the other source had surprised her. Greatly.

The hall outside the gym was lined with backpacks that students had been told to leave because the bleachers would be crowded. Suddenly, Caleb squatted down and started to retie his shoelaces. "Go ahead, Ms. B. I'll just be a moment."

Ms. B continued toward the gym, knowing precisely why Caleb told her to go ahead. He didn't want to be seen entering the gym with her. Caleb was a clever boy and mature for his age. Last year he began showing her articles and videos about eSports. At first Ms. B had been doubtful about eSports in school, much the way Principal Summers was that morning in the computer lab. But Caleb was relentless and finally got her to agree to help him with the Providia grant. Even now, she was amazed that they were able to get the computers for free.

And that brought her thoughts back to Zach. Ms. B had known boys like him. Boys who worried her because they seemed perpetually lost, lonely, suffering from poor impulse control and low self-esteem. Boys who were unaffiliated with anyone and anything at school. But what Zach had done with his notebook was oddly encouraging. The work was so careful. So precise. The corners of the hollowed-out rectangle for the phone were perfectly square. The sides meticulously trimmed. The pages stuck together with just enough glue, not a single extra drop or glob. The work revealed a level of care and craftsmanship that she never would have associated with him. When she asked what he'd been doing with the phone, he said something about a video game. That made her think that he might be a good fit for the eSports club.

Emma sat with the class shoulder to shoulder and thigh to thigh high up in the gym bleachers. She put her hoodie beside her to save a place for Caleb. Everyone around her was sneaking peeks at their phones. Students were supposed to leave their devices in their lockers, but hardly anyone did. And in a crowded assembly like this, it wasn't like teachers were going to hike up through the packed bleachers to take the phones away.

Down on the gym floor, Principal Summers stood at a microphone, urging the students to squeeze in as tightly as possible. "We need to get the whole school in here. So if you've brought anything with you, please keep it on your lap."

"Hey, Emma, didn't you hear what Principal Summers just said?" someone asked.

Emma instantly recognized the voice. Her stomach clenched. It was just her luck that the person sitting on the other side of her hoodie was Mackenzie "Mistress of Microaggressions" Storrs.

Emma imagined asking, since when did Mackenzie care what Principal Summers said? But she knew that she wouldn't, because it would lead to the sort of confrontation that she dreaded. Now Mackenzie's BFF, Isabella Reed, added her two cents. "Let's see who she's saving it for."

A chill swept through Emma. If those two saw who she was saving the seat for, she was certain to become a target for their ridicule. Some kids liked Caleb, but others called him a suck-up and Extra Credit Caleb behind his back. He reminded Emma of her older sister, Sarah, who as a senior the year before had been voted most likely to succeed. For that reason alone, some kids disliked Sarah. Caleb always came to school neatly dressed, and Emma thought he was charming. In fact, she was secretly thrilled that he asked her to save a seat for him. But now she feared the teasing Mackenzie would heap on her for doing that.

The gym doors began to open. Emma caught her breath.

But it was Zach, not Caleb, who came in. Sitting a few rows in front of Emma, Crosby gave Gavin a nudge and said loudly enough for everyone around them to hear, "Let's get him to sit in front of us."

Emma knew that meant trouble. Zach was slightly bigger than Crosby, but that didn't stop Crosby from picking on him. Emma suspected that the only reason Crosby got away with it was because Gavin had his back. That was something new. Until this year, Robbie Jones had been Gavin's best friend. They were two of the best players on the football team and were always together in the hall and at lunch. But over the summer, Robbie moved to Franklin to play football on their middle school team.

Emma watched as Crosby ordered the kids sitting in front of him to make room. With Gavin sitting next to him, the kids instantly scooched apart. "Hey, Wack, sit here!" Crosby shouted. "We saved you a seat."

Zach was already coming up the bleachers. But when he heard Crosby call to him, he stopped and appeared to cower.

"You heard me, Wack," Crosby growled, and pointed at the space in front of him. "I want you here."

Zach hung his head and climbed up to the spot where Crosby wanted him to sit. Emma felt bad. For as long as she could remember, there had been anti-bullying programs in school. Teachers talked about it in class, and there wasn't a hall you could walk down without seeing anti-bullying posters. If Crosby didn't get the message, it was because he didn't want to.

The gym doors opened again, and Caleb came in. He stopped at the bottom of the bleachers and scanned the crowd.

Emma knew he was looking for her. She yearned to wave, but the thought of what Mackenzie might say terrified her. She was certain that if she let Caleb sit next to her, Mackenzie would take a picture and post it along with some malicious comment. So she ducked down and hoped Caleb wouldn't see her.

◯

Caleb had never seen the gym bleachers so packed. The assembly was about to begin, and when he couldn't find Emma in the crowd, he sat down in a bleacher aisle. Kids weren't supposed to sit in the aisles, but no one seemed to care much about rules anymore.

While Principal Summers told the students to quiet down and get ready for "a delightful and inspiring assembly," Caleb thought back to what had just happened in the hall. When he told Ms. B about Crosby's plan to cheat on the geometry test, she said she already knew about it. But how? Who could have told her before he had? He gazed at the many red and white football banners that hung on the gym walls: Middle School State champions. Conference Champions. State Runner-Up. It wasn't easy to feel delighted or inspired about school now that they'd lost their football team.

"Okay, everyone," Principal Summers shouted enthusiastically, "let's give it up for one of our most famous Ironville alumni, Harry the Hoopster!"

Out of the boys' locker room came a skinny, bow-legged,

gray-haired guy wearing long white basket shorts and a baggy white jersey. He was dribbling two basketballs at once. The bleachers went silent. Caleb imagined that most of the crowd was thinking: *Is this for real?*

Caleb had never heard of Harry the Hoopster, who looked old and bony enough to be his grandfather. Scratch that. Harry looked ancient enough to be Caleb's *great*-grandfather. His wrinkled and saggy skin was practically the color of milk. He was so pale, it looked like he hadn't been out in the sun since the invention of *Pac-Man*. Tufts of hair poked out around the neckline of his jersey like small white weeds.

Caleb understood that the school wanted to keep students engaged now that the football program had been cut. But was hiring an old coot who could barely stand up straight the best way to do that? Just then, one of the basketballs Harry was dribbling bounced away, and he had to chase it. Snickers rippled across the bleachers.

It took a while for Harry to dribble both balls over to the microphone. Then into the mic he said, "Why did the basketball coach want a frog on the squad? Because he heard it had a great jump shot!"

The joke was met with groans, but that didn't stop the old guy. "You hear about the basketball player who signed up for arts and crafts? He wanted to learn how to make baskets!"

There were more groans from the crowd. But Harry plowed forward, spinning a basketball on his finger, then on his elbow, and then on his head. All the while he talked about character building, sharing, caring, and kindness. Caleb wondered if, with the football program gone, someone thought it would be a good idea to encourage kids to focus on basketball instead. So they hired old Harry to get everyone psyched up while he impressed them with his mastery of basketball spinning.

It was almost beyond pathetic.

Suddenly, there were murmurs and giggles all around Caleb. Phones were vibrating, and kids were sneaking peeks. Caleb looked over the shoulder of the boy in front of him. Someone had AirDropped a GIF of a bony old man wearing a skimpy Speedo and flexing his scrawny muscles.

The crowd spent the rest of the assembly looking at their phones. At first Caleb was surprised that Principal Summers didn't try to stop them. Unless she, too, had decided the assembly was a mistake. And as long as the kids were occupied by their phones, at least they were being quiet.

The presentation ended, and Harry the Hoopster asked if anyone had a question. An awkward silence followed. The only sound was the bleachers creaking. Then Crosby leaned forward and whispered something into Zach's ear. When Zach shook his head, Crosby made a threatening fist and held it low where only Zach and those around him could see.

Zach reluctantly raised his hand. "Mr. Hoopster, sir. Don't you think there should be a law against old guys wearing shorts?"

○

The assembly was over and Zach was in trouble again. Back at her desk in her classroom, Ms. B wondered why she worried about him. He certainly wasn't the only kid in school who got into mischief. But during the assembly, Ms. B was looking up at the bleachers when she saw Crosby whisper into Zach's ear. Of course, she couldn't hear what Crosby said. But a moment later Zach asked that silly question. So she had reason to feel suspicious. Ms. B knew that Zach could be foolish at times, but she doubted he'd ask that question in front of the whole school if he wasn't forced to. Deep down, Ms. B felt a connection with Zach. She, too, had been picked on at that age. Only in her case, there'd been no one to help her deal with it.

Just then, she looked out the classroom door and saw Caleb pass in the hallway. "Caleb?" she called. "Could I speak to you?"

He came in. Ms. B had gotten to know him well during the past year: First while he pestered her to take the idea of an eSports club seriously. And then while they worked together on the grant proposal. He could be so determined and persuasive, and she'd come to believe he could do anything he set his mind to. Besides, they'd shared confidences. She felt she could trust him. He'd told her about Crosby's plan to cheat on the geometry test. In her opinion, Caleb Arnett was a reliable boy.

"Looks like your dream of an eSports club is about to come true," she said to him. "Congratulations."

Caleb beamed. "Amazing, huh?"

Ms. B nodded. "Can I ask you a favor?"

"Uh, sure."

"Would you try to get Zach Cook to come to the informational meeting this afternoon? I think it would be good for him."

It was sixth period and Zach was relieved to be in the safe confines of the library where he didn't have to worry about Ratface Crosby bothering him. Snot rockets like Ratface would rather lick toilets than be seen in the library.

It had been a stressful day for Zach. After Ratface forced him to ask that dumb question during the assembly, he'd spent most of the morning in the office waiting for Principal Summers to mete out his punishment—she'd given a stern lecture and a week of lunchtime detentions sitting at a table facing teachers. He and his fellow prisoners weren't allowed to speak. They couldn't even rest their heads on their arms. Was there any punishment worse than having to look at teachers across a table for forty minutes?

So it was a relief to be in the library during a free period. Zach had taken over two PCs. On one he played *Minecraft*, one of the few games the school district's filters allowed. On the other, he watched surfing videos.

Then, out of nowhere, Extra Credit Caleb sat down beside him. "*Minecraft* and surfing, huh?" the kid said. "You see on Twitch about people building the Taj Mahal on *MC*? The details are amazing!"

Zach wasn't sure what to do. He and Caleb had been in school together since kindergarten, but they'd hardly ever spoken. Zach paused the game and glanced around the library. Was this a prank? Were Caleb's friends hiding in the stacks, watching or recording them? Meanwhile, Caleb pointed at the other computer screen. "You into surfing? Cool."

Why is Caleb Arnett trying to be friendly? Zach wondered. *What does he want? Is he just going to sit there and talk the whole period?*

Zach began to blink and bounce his knees rapidly. At a loss for what to do, he turned to the other keyboard and pulled up "Biggest wave ever surfed." He and Caleb watched the tiny image of extreme surfer Marc Nguyen scudding down the face of a giant blue wall of curling water at Nazaré.

"Biggest wave ever?" Caleb said. "Sick."

Once again, Zach looked around to check if anyone was watching. But he also knew Caleb wasn't the type to play tricks or make fun of someone. He was one of those kids whose hair was always neatly trimmed. His shirt was always tucked in and his sneakers looked new and barely scuffed. He was too much of a do-gooder to be openly mean.

"So listen," Caleb said. "Know the eSports club Ms. B is starting?"

Zach frowned. *eSports club?*

"Remember the morning announcements?" Caleb caught himself and grinned. "You were busy watching your phone in that notebook, right?"

Zach felt his face turn warm with embarrassment. He recalled how Caleb had come back to the classroom while Ms. B was chewing him out about the notebook.

"What were you watching anyway?" Caleb asked.

"*Good War* tutorials," Zach said, barely above a whisper.

"That's what I'm playing!" Caleb gushed. "Don't you love how smooth the gameplay is? And how the developers actually care about keeping it balanced? Real boots-on-the-ground combat. Not one of those dumb FPS extravaganzas set in the year AD six million with all that made-up futuristic crap, you know?"

Zach nodded. It sounded like Caleb knew what he was talking about.

"Know what would be super cool?" Caleb asked excitedly. "If that's the game the eSports club plays."

Fat chance, Zach thought. *The Good War* was rated M. *No way would it ever get through the district web filter.* And he still didn't understand why Caleb was telling him this. Zach didn't like school, and he didn't like clubs. Why would he like a school club?

"Want to give it a try?" Caleb asked.

Why is he trying to get me to be in a club? Zach wondered. Caleb had never shown any interest in him before. Normally, Caleb was interested only in things that gave him a chance to excel and show everyone he was the best.

"I mean," Caleb went on, "don't you at least want to check out those Providia X-Masters? They freaking sound awesome."

Zach had to admit that Caleb seemed sincere. It was so rare that anyone at school wanted anything to do with him. He said he'd think about it.

○

"So, Ms. B caught you," Gavin said to Crosby. School had just ended, and they were walking to the computer lab to see what the new eSports club was all about.

"She didn't catch me," Crosby muttered angrily. Twenty minutes ago, in the middle of the geometry test, Ms. B suddenly told Crosby to join her out in the hall. There she asked to see the sides of his fingers, where he'd written the formulas in tiny letters and numbers. Then she told him to go down to the boys' room and scrub his hands.

"Then how did she know?" Gavin asked.

Good question, Crosby thought. There was only one person he'd told about his plan to cheat, and that was Gavin. Crosby didn't want to believe that Gavin would rat on him, but then, he didn't actually know Gavin that well, did he? It was only for the past month that Gavin had let Crosby hang out with him, and the guy never wanted to talk about anything personal.

"Somebody must've told her," Crosby said, curious to see how Gavin would react. A bunch of sixth graders were gathered in the middle of the hall ahead of them, but when they saw Gavin approaching, they quickly moved to the side. Crosby enjoyed walking with Gavin. Nobody, not even the eighth graders, dared mess with the big red-haired seventh grader. Crosby liked to bask in the glow of power that seemed to radiate from the guy.

"Oh yeah?" Gavin said. "Who do you think told her?"

Does Gavin really not know? Crosby wondered. *Or is he just pretending in order to throw me off the scent?*

○

Emma was walking toward the computer lab when someone behind her said, "Hey." She turned. It was Caleb. "Thought you were going to save me a seat at the assembly," he said.

Emma felt her face flush. "I did. I saw you come into the

gym but you didn't see me." That was sort of true. Though, with Mackenzie and Isabella there, Emma hadn't tried to be seen.

Caleb's eyebrows dipped. "I thought I looked everywhere."

"Maybe you didn't see me because it was so crowded," Emma said lamely. For the next few steps, neither of them spoke. Emma felt bad. Surely Caleb suspected she wasn't being entirely truthful. *When in doubt, change the subject*, she thought. "Ms. B said you had something to do with the eSports club?"

Caleb explained how last spring he'd collected a bunch of news stories about schools that were launching clubs and showed them to Ms. B. And how he wrote the grant proposal for the new computers.

"*You* wrote it?" Emma asked, surprised that Caleb, who'd been a sixth grader last spring, had done something like that.

"Sure," Caleb said with a grin. "I mean, I got some help from Ms. B and my parents. But the thing is, the people who read those grant proposals have no idea how old you are."

Emma was impressed. Writing a grant proposal sounded complicated. But it was just the sort of thing Caleb *would* do. Suddenly, Caleb leaned close to her. "Know what? Maybe it would be better if you didn't tell anyone about the grant," he said, barely above a whisper. "I already have a reputation for being a suck-up."

Emma felt honored that he'd confided in her. She wondered if it was because they'd partnered on a project in art the year before. The assignment was to make spray-paint landscapes. Most of the kids in the class just used the materials the art teacher provided, but as always, Caleb wanted to do more. Emma found his enthusiasm infectious and was happy to be his accomplice. While the rest of the class did traditional landscapes like forests and mountains, Caleb suggested they do an underwater scene with corals and fish, a shipwreck and sea turtles. They'd researched the idea together. Then Caleb found foam brushes and palette knives, while Emma got specially colored spray paints. Together they turned an everyday art project into something unusual. And in the process, she'd developed a little crush on him.

By now they were nearing the computer lab. "So, uh, you going to the gaming meeting?" Caleb asked. "You're a gamer?"

"Who isn't?" Emma said, feeling proud because she thought that sounded clever.

Caleb grinned. "Yeah, right?"

It felt good that Caleb appreciated her humor. Most of the time, the only person who got to appreciate it was Emma herself. Because she rarely said such things out loud.

"You psyched to play on those Providias?" Caleb asked.

"I'm psyched to play on a fast connection," Emma said. "The joke in our house is that our internet's so slow that . . ."

They walked a few more steps. Caleb glanced at her. "So slow that what?"

"We don't know," Emma said. "We're still waiting for it to load."

A laugh burst out of Caleb's chest. "Good one!"

Emma felt herself glow inside.

When they got to the computer lab, the only other people there were Ms. B and that new boy, Nathan. Caleb and Emma sat at the near end of the long table where the new PCs had been set up. Ms. B stood by the door, waiting to see who'd arrive next.

"Know anyone else who's coming?" Caleb whispered to Emma. She shook her head, but she was thrilled that Caleb kept asking her questions.

When the computer lab door opened and Gavin and Crosby came in, the smile on Ms. B's lips shrank to a thin flat line. Emma doubted that either of the boys noticed. Crosby immediately went over to one of the Providia X-Masters. He looked at the big screen and then ducked down to check out the tower under the table. "Sick," he said loudly.

Meanwhile, Gavin gave Emma and Caleb an impassive look. Then he and Crosby sat down at the far end of the table and stashed their backpacks under their chairs. Maybe it was just her imagination, but Emma got the feeling that battle lines were being drawn.

○

So far it had been a good day for Caleb. He helped stop Crosby from cheating on the geometry test, and the eSports club, which he had worked so hard on, had become a reality. Of course, he couldn't have done it without Ms. B's help, and he felt he owed her something for that. So if Zach actually showed up for the club, Caleb would feel like he'd paid her back.

Each time the computer lab door opened, Caleb watched Ms. B turn her head with an expectant look, but so far, the person they really wanted to see hadn't arrived. When Mackenzie and Isabella came in, Caleb felt himself wince inwardly. When he'd pictured what the club would be like, he hadn't imagined the mean girls, or guys like Gavin and Crosby, joining. Caleb's afternoons were already packed. Almost every day after school he had an activity. Yearbook, debate club, piano lessons, Chinese club. For an instant, he wondered if he wanted to be in the eSports club with kids like that. But he quickly pushed the thought out of his mind. The club was his idea, and it was about gaming, not about personalities. He was well aware that Crosby and Mackenzie were the kinds of kids who called him Extra Credit Caleb behind his back, but maybe, if they all gamed together, it would change.

Meanwhile, Ms. B still kept glancing at the door. Caleb found himself feeling disappointed that Zach hadn't shown up. And it wasn't just about paying Ms. B back for helping him create the eSports club. Caleb had been surprised that afternoon while hanging out with Zach in the library. Zach might have been full of fidgets and tics, but there was also something clever and sincere about him. He didn't try to act cool. He didn't pretend to be anything except himself. Caleb found that interesting. In a way, he and Zach were opposites.

The door opened again, and a kid named Tyler Phillips came in. All Caleb knew of Tyler was that he was a practical joker who tended to fool around a lot. When Tyler saw the new computers, he widened his eyes like a prospector who'd just found gold. "Man, this is amazing!" he gushed. "I've never seen one of these things in real life."

Ms. B pushed open the computer lab door and glanced out into the hall. Caleb sensed she couldn't wait much longer to begin the meeting. The kids were getting restless. Ms. B let the door close and faced the group. She worked a smile onto her lips. "I'm so glad you all decided to come. I really think we're going—"

She stopped and turned her head. Zach was peeking in the window. Ms. B went to the door and opened it. Zach stuck his nose in like a wary mouse sniffing cheese in a mousetrap.

"Come in, Zach," Ms. B said. Wearing a backpack and carrying his skateboard, Zach took a tentative step, then stopped. His eyes darted around as if he was trying to assess the possible level of danger in the room. From somewhere on Gavin's side of the table came a loud snort. Zach stiffened.

"Just take a seat, Zach." Ms. B put a hand on his shoulder and guided him deeper into the room as if she was worried that at any second he would change his mind and scamper away.

Caleb watched Zach take a seat in a corner, about as far from Gavin and Crosby as he could get. There had been a time when Caleb would have been satisfied that Zach showed up, because it would mean he'd paid Ms. B back. But with Gavin and his pals there, Caleb felt a different sensation. An unexpected one that made him uncomfortable. He was worried that all he'd done was help feed Zach to the wolves.

When Mackenzie and Isabella entered the computer lab, Emma cringed. They were the last people on earth she wanted to be in a club with. But the more she thought about it, the more she wanted to game with Caleb. And besides, now it was too late to leave. Ms. B began the informational meeting by saying she hoped that someday they'd join the Middle School eSports League and play against other schools, but Ironville didn't have the funds, so for now, they would just have two teams play each other at one game.

"Think of this semester as the beta test for the club," she said. "Today we can figure out how we want to organize, what the teams will be, and what game you'll play. Does anyone have a suggestion?"

The new kid, Nathan, raised his hand. "Can we pick a game rated M?"

Play an M-rated game in school? Emma thought. It was the kind of question only a new kid would ask. The district web filter would never permit it. She expected Ms. B to shoot the idea down.

But Ms. B said, "Which one?"

"The Good War!" Tyler blurted before anyone else had time to react.

"Yeah!" Crosby agreed with a fist pump.

The Good War was one of the hottest games out. Emma had played it several times. It was easy to learn and the action was fast-paced and fun. But it was rated M for violence and animated blood.

"So is that okay, Ms. B?" Tyler asked hopefully.

Not in a million years, Emma thought. And yet the others seemed to be holding their breaths while Ms. B googled some reviews of the game.

Waiting for the inevitable "no way," Emma watched Nathan press his lips together and slide down in his chair.

She got the feeling that *TGW* wasn't the game he'd wanted to suggest when he'd asked about the M rating. But being new at school, he probably thought it best not to argue. He was a nice-looking boy with longish brown hair and a thin, straight nose. He held himself erect when he walked, like a soldier marching.

Meanwhile, at her desk, Ms. B appeared to be lost in thought. Then she nodded. "It doesn't sound like anything you probably haven't played before. So yes, why not?"

"What about the district web filter?" Emma asked.

"This is a club, not school," Ms. B said.

"All right!" Tyler and Crosby cheered in unison and high-fived. Emma was truly amazed.

Next they discussed the format of play and settled on nine rounds per match, with the first team to win five rounds considered that day's winner. The same would go for the semester. They'd meet for nine weeks. The first team to win five matches would be the semester champions.

Just then, Emma felt something press against her thigh. She looked down. Caleb was slipping her a note . . . made of paper. *How retro!* she thought as she unfolded it. On it Caleb had written: NOT ME. YOU.

Huh? Emma had no idea what that meant. She scowled at him. Caleb nodded back as if the answer would be clear soon enough.

When Ms. B suggested that they choose captains, Crosby said, "Gavin."

Gavin's forehead bunched doubtfully, but Tyler and Mackenzie gave thumbs up to show they agreed. Next, Ms. B turned to Emma and Caleb's end of the table. Now Emma understood the note Caleb had given her. He wanted her to be the captain of their side. But how could he already know what the teams would be? And when had she ever been the captain of anything?

Ms. B's eyes settled on Caleb as if she expected him to be captain. Emma suspected that Caleb wanted to keep a low profile. Still, being captain meant Emma would stand out and be in charge, things she always tried to avoid. She was the kind of person who wouldn't even post a selfie for fear of not getting any likes. She could already imagine the nasty "Who Does She Think She Is?" comments Mackenzie and Isabella would post. But Caleb had asked her to do it, and he was probably already disappointed in her because he thought she hadn't saved him a seat in the assembly. Did she really want to disappoint him twice in the same day?

Emma raised her hand. For an instant, Ms. B couldn't hide the look of surprise on her face, but she quickly recovered. "All right, Emma. You'll be the other captain. Now go ahead and pick your squads."

In Caleb's mind, there was no doubt that Gavin, Crosby, Tyler, Mackenzie, and Isabella would be one squad because they were all sort of in the same social crowd. And he, Emma, Zach, and that new kid, Nathan, would be the other squad because they weren't in that crowd.

The problem was that for most of the meeting Zach kept his hoodie pulled so low over his head that his face was mostly hidden. His feet were tapping nonstop, and his knees bounced rapidly. His hands were jammed as deep as they could go into his pockets, and he kept sniffing loudly. It was obvious to Caleb that Zach didn't want to be there and that once he left, he wasn't coming back.

Ms. B had everyone set up gaming accounts, and then the meeting ended. The first match would be the following week. Now kids were leaving to catch the late bus. Caleb expected Zach to blast out of the computer lab, but instead he dawdled in the back of the room. Was it because Zach didn't want to go out into the hallway while Crosby was around?

Caleb gathered his things. He'd just pulled on his backpack when he heard Ms. B clear her throat. Her eyes darted at Zach and then back to Caleb. She gave him a look that said *Try to get Zach to join.*

No sooner did Emma volunteer to be captain than she regretted it. Especially with Mackenzie and Isabella on the opposite squad. She decided that she would talk to Caleb on the late bus, but when she left to catch it, he was still hanging around the computer lab.

On the late bus, Gavin, Crosby, Makenzie, and Isabella were sitting in the back. The only open seats were right in front of them. When Mackenzie saw Emma, she narrowed her eyes as if she'd already thought of the meanest thing she could possibly say and couldn't wait to deliver it.

Emma felt a shiver, then chastised herself for being afraid. *If I already know that Mackenzie doesn't like me, why do I care so much about what she thinks and says?* she asked herself. Was it because snarky remarks hurt no matter who said them? Meanwhile, she'd been the last to get on the bus, and the driver was watching her in the rearview mirror, waiting for her to find a seat so that they could go. Emma reluctantly went down the aisle. Mackenzie looked like a viper coiling to strike. She reminded Emma of a young Excella Gionne from *Resident Evil*. Emma felt her stomach begin to knot. But then she saw Gavin sitting across the aisle from Mackenzie. His eyes met hers, but unlike Mackenzie's, his looked sort of sad. Emma's and Gavin's parents had known each other since before she and Gavin were born. Their fathers had been best friends in high school and then worked in the steel mill together. When she and Gavin were little, they had been playmates. They'd even shared a playpen at times. But in fifth grade they'd drifted apart. It had been years since they'd said more than hi to each other.

Gavin's father hurt his back a few months ago and had been on disability ever since. Emma's father said Mr. Morgenstern's recovery was going slowly because he could get to physical therapy in Franklin only once a week. Was that why Gavin looked sad?

"How's your dad doing?" she asked him.

Gavin had just unwrapped a piece of candy and popped it into his mouth. With his cheek bulging, he blinked at her in surprise. Probably because these days he and Emma barely acknowledged each other at school. "Oh, uh . . . not so good."

"Sorry to hear that, Gavin," Emma said, and sat down. As the bus pulled away from the curb, she waited for Mackenzie's comment, but it never came. Was it because whatever mean thing Mackenzie was planning to say would sound stupid now that Emma had been friendly to Gavin? A smile crept across Emma's face. In the never-ending battle against the Mistress of Microaggressions, she felt like she'd scored a small victory.

"I'm not doing this for Ms. B," Caleb said. He and Zach had just left school and Zach asked if Ms. B told Caleb to walk home with him. Zach knew that Caleb didn't live in that direction. He lived over near Cardinal Lake, the "nice" part of town. As if any part of Ironville were actually "nice."

"So why are you going this way?" Zach asked.

"It's hard to explain," Caleb said.

Zach doubted that. He suspected that Caleb was lying about not being asked by Ms. B. Or maybe Caleb's parents had told him to be friendly to Zach. It wouldn't be the first time a kid from school had suddenly decided to be Zach's friend. Out of the blue, someone would invite Zach over to their house. The playdate would feel awkward. Zach almost always got the feeling that the kid didn't really want him there. The date would always include a snack in the kitchen with the kid's mother hovering close by, pretending not to listen in. Zach would feel like he was under a microscope with everything he said and did being scrutinized. He always suspected that his own mother had asked the other boy's mother if she'd arrange the get-together.

Zach doubted it was any different with Extra Credit Caleb. He was pretty sure this was all about scoring brownie points with Ms. B. But that was about to end. They'd gotten to the old stone wall. This was as far as Zach wanted Caleb to go. He dropped his skateboard to the street, implying that he planned to skateboard the rest of the way home.

"So really, Zach, what do you think about the club?" Caleb asked.

There it is, Zach thought. There was no reason why Caleb would give a hoot what he thought of the club. No reason why he should care if Zach joined or not.

"Listen, Zach," Caleb went on. "You have as much right to be in that club as anyone else. I mean, if those idiots Crosby and Gavin are keeping you from joining . . ."

Zach was about to get on the skateboard but he stopped. Was it *that* obvious that the reason he wasn't going to join the eSports club was because of Ratface Crosby and that crowd?

"Just think about it tonight, okay?" Caleb said.

A chipmunk scurried along the stone wall and vanished into a crevice. Zach was baffled. He didn't know what to make of Caleb's suggestion.

"See you tomorrow," Caleb said, and turned away. Zach stepped onto the deck of his board and pushed off, but after a dozen yards, he did a frontside slide and looked back. Caleb was walking briskly, as if he was in a hurry. As if he'd just taken care of one task but still had others to complete. Zach thought about what he'd just said. The truth was, playing *The Good*

War on a Providia X-Master with a fast connection was super tempting. Gaming without lags or screen stuttering would be awesome. And more importantly, did he really want to live the rest of his life in fear?

○

Dinner that night was boneless, skinless, tasteless free-range chicken, kale and quinoa salad, and sweet potatoes. Just once Caleb wished he could sink his teeth into a bacon cheeseburger. But his parents would rather starve than eat anything tasty and unhealthy, and they expected the same of him. Also expected of him tonight was his daily report. In addition to doing the dinner dishes, recycling, flossing, practicing piano, walking Cooper, and picking up her poop, Caleb was expected to recount for his parents what happened at school each day.

"Have you found a photographer for the yearbook?" his mother asked.

Caleb was the yearbook photo editor. If he did well, he could look forward to being the managing editor next year. For the past few weeks he'd been interviewing photographers for the student portraits. "I think so. He's new and way less expensive than the others."

Caleb's father took off his thick black-framed glasses and cleaned them with a napkin. "Less expensive isn't always better. How do you know he'll do a good job?"

"I thought his portfolio looked cool," Caleb said. "Besides, Ms. Dean, the yearbook advisor, says there isn't enough money in the budget for the photographer they used last year."

"And how was the first meeting of the eSports club?" his mother asked. The meeting had only been announced that morning, but his mother already knew about it. Caleb wasn't surprised. Both his mother and father were plugged into what he called the Parental Hovernet. The Hovernet was an aggregation of school announcements, teacher-parent emails, texts, rumors . . . anything that helped helicopter parents like his keep tabs on what their kids were doing on a daily, if not minute-to-minute, basis.

Caleb said that the meeting had gone well.

"I think it's wonderful that you did that for the school," his mother said. "But I hope it doesn't mean that you're just going to play video games from now on."

"Hey, don't knock it," Mr. Arnett said. "If he gets good enough, he could get a college scholarship."

"The top players make millions," Caleb added.

"Are you really thinking about becoming a professional gamer?" his mother asked with a frown.

Caleb didn't need to be a professional gamer. Writing the grant proposal and getting the Providia computers and fast connection was good for the eSports club and for the school and had been a challenge for him. Of course, it would also look good on his transcript, where his one glaring weakness was in sports.

But despite what he'd accomplished, Caleb didn't feel satisfied. The brief glimpse of school life through Zach's eyes that afternoon was nagging at him. There was definitely more to Zach than the weird kid you saw in the halls walking backward or making bizarre noises. Caleb was surprised to discover that it bothered him that any kid had to be afraid to join a club, or to get on a bus. It was bad enough that every time they had a lockdown drill, they were reminded that the world was full of maniacs with semiautomatic weapons who might break into school and kill a bunch of students. Why should Zach, or any other kid, have to live in fear of the people who were *already* in school?

○

Crosby was psyched about the eSports club. He'd been playing *The Good War* for a couple of months and already knew the maps. He even knew a few lesser-known spots and glitches that would give his squad an advantage in the game. And having that advantage would make Gavin happy.

When Crosby first got into *TGW*, he played against random gamers based on their Elo ratings. But over time he'd gotten to know some players and considered them friends. Now they squadded up when they saw each other online. They even had their own private Discord channel to chat. One guy he particularly liked had the handle 88Rising. He was a good listener.

"My girlfriend's annoying sister, Mary, came over for dinner," Crosby told 88Rising that night. Crosby didn't have a girlfriend. But 88Rising's deep voice made Crosby think he was in his twenties, so Crosby pretended to be older. In reality, his aunt Mary had come over because Crosby's mom was seriously ill. Aunt Mary was a nurse in Franklin, but three or four nights a week she drove a couple of hours to Ironville to cook dinner and help with his mom's care.

"Oh yeah? What's the sister's story, CrossBow?" 88Rising asked. CrossBow was Crosby's handle.

"She's always going on about women's rights, and how women are oppressed, and junk like that."

"Oh yeah, that type," 88Rising said dismissively.

"So during dinner I mentioned eSports," Crosby said. "I mean, I was just making conversation, you know? But Mary instantly goes off. Like how can my girlfriend sit by while I play video games? Doesn't she know gamers are all anti-women? Hasn't she ever heard of Gamergate?"

"Gamer what?" 88Rising said.

"I didn't know what it was, either," Crosby said. "So I looked it up. It was this thing that happened years ago where some jerks got into a fight with a couple of female developers. It blew up because these guys called in fake terrorist threats on the women, and the police raided their houses."

"They swatted them?" 88Rising asked.

"Yup," Crosby said. "So some people started to think that male gamers were weirdos who spent most of their time attacking women."

"That's lame, bro," 88Rising said.

"Right!" Crosby agreed. "But does my girlfriend defend me? No! She stares at me like, is that true? And I'm like, no way. And Mary goes, just wait. She tells my girlfriend that the longer I'm in that 'misogynistic gaming culture' the more chance there is that I'll end up being a hard-core woman-hater."

Those were the exact words his aunt Mary had used.

"Misogy . . . what?" 88Rising asked.

"Yeah, right?" Crosby chuckled. That's what he liked about

88Rising. He didn't pretend to be a brainiac. He just wanted to play games and have fun. "So, the next thing I know, my girlfriend's saying maybe I shouldn't be gaming so much. Can you believe that?"

That was actually what Crosby's mother had said.

"Hell yeah," 88Rising said. "Welcome to the real world, CrossBow. Women, immigrants, minorities . . . they all want to blame white males for everything that's wrong in their lives."

By now it was after midnight, and Crosby was wiped. He'd played nearly five hours of *TGW*, and his wrists were beginning to ache. He told 88Rising he was getting off and would be back tomorrow. 88Rising always signed off with RaHoWa 14/88, whatever that meant.

Crosby crawled into bed. Even though his eyelids felt heavy, he found himself thinking about what had happened that day in geometry. *Could Gavin really be the one who ratted on me?* It killed Crosby to think that. He wanted Gavin to be his friend. He *needed* Gavin to be his friend. But if Gavin hadn't told Ms. B about his plan to cheat, how had she known? Who else could have told her?

Crosby fell asleep pondering that mystery. Nearly four hours later, in the middle of the night, he suddenly woke. The answer had come to him.

PART
TWO

WEEK FOUR

GAVIN'S SQUAD: 3

EMMA'S SQUAD: 0

They were in tight quarters in *TGW*. As Emma crept past the gray concrete walls of the bunker, she could sense a shoot-out looming.

"Careful," Caleb cautioned. "This is a choke point. Not an easy angle to push."

"No prob, bro. I'm feelin' good," said Nathan. "Just got a new sight for my Springfield '03."

"I'm in the bunker now," Emma said into her headset. "Where are those guys?"

"They just passed back through their spawn," said Zach. "They're headed for the stairs."

Emma felt a buzz of excitement as she joined the rest of the squad taking cover near the top of the stairs. The eSports club had competed three times over the past month, and so far, Gavin's squad had won every match. But today they were tied at four rounds each. Going into this final clash, Emma felt that her squad had a chance to win.

Just as Zach predicted, Gavin's squad came up the stairs.

"Here they come! We can close this game right now," Nathan yelled into his headset.

"Wait. Just wait," Caleb, ever the cautious one, begged. But it was too late. Nathan began shooting, and the rest of them joined in blasting Gavin's squad, who quickly dived for cover.

"How is he not dead?" Emma heard Nathan yell.

"Zach, why is your knife out?" Caleb cried.

"Gotcha, ya Nazi bastids!" Nathan shouted so loud, it distorted in Emma's headset.

"Language, Nathan," Ms. B warned. Normally the other squad couldn't hear what they said online, but when Nathan got fired up, and shouted, everyone in the room could hear. And Nathan had good reason to be excited. He'd just clinched the round with an amazing triple kill! Emma's squad won the match!

Emma pulled off her headset, and she and her squad shared fist bumps and big grins. Even Zach joined in, with none of his usual jitters. Everyone patted Nathan on the back. Emma was especially pumped. Over the past month she had discovered that she really enjoyed being part of the squad. She'd been on teams before, like soccer and softball, but she always felt insignificant because she wasn't a standout player. But on the eSports squad she was one of only four. Her play accounted for one quarter of the team's effort. And being captain gave her role even more importance.

Meanwhile, across the table, Gavin's squad leaned back in their chairs, pulled off their headsets, and looked grumpy.

"You know, my brother says they weren't Nazis," Mackenzie said sourly. Today Emma's squad had been the Allies and Gavin's were the Axis.

"Come again?" Emma said. Mackenzie's comment seemed to come out of nowhere. Almost. Knowing Mackenzie, she always had to have the last word.

"We were talking about it," Mackenzie went on. "When you're the Axis side, you're the Wehrmacht. The German army. They weren't the same as the Nazis. They weren't trying to wipe out all the Jews. They were just doing their duty. You really should be more careful about who you call a Nazi."

Emma's squad fell silent. No one knew how to respond. But it felt like their triumph had been muted. Mackenzie smiled. It seemed to Emma that if Mackenzie's side couldn't win the match, the next best thing was to make sure the other squad didn't get to enjoy their victory.

As captain of her squad, Emma wanted her players to feel good. She wished she could think of something to say to retaliate. But even if she did, she doubted she'd say it. Mackenzie was just an okay gamer. Emma was better. But she still felt intimidated by Mackenzie, and by Isabella, who'd dropped out of the club after the first week. Emma was still afraid of the hurtful things they might say if she got on their radar. She might have been squad captain, but once a match was over, she was still the same old anxious Emma.

Because the seventh grade wouldn't study European history until next year, they hadn't covered World War II in any detail. So it was curious to Ms. B to hear what the members of the club had learned or heard outside of school. She was surprised today when Mackenzie lectured the others on the difference between the German soldiers and the Nazis. Ms. B wasn't sure about that, and would have to check. Still, she thought Principal Summers would be pleased to learn that there was an educational aspect to the eSports club.

But that wasn't the only good news Ms. B planned to share with the principal. At lunch in the teachers' room today, Mr. Parnes, who taught language arts, announced that he'd been nominated to thank her. Ms. B had looked up from her Tupperware container of chopped brussels sprouts and kale. "You're welcome, Mr. Parnes. But for what?"

"The change in Zach Cook," said Mr. Parnes. He was a gaunt, stooped fellow whose entire wardrobe consisted of plaid shirts and khakis. Shakespeare was his passion, and each year he directed the school play.

"It's not like he's suddenly become a model student," added Ms. Orlean, who taught social studies. "But we've all noticed a change for the better."

"You've given him the opportunity to stand out," Mr. Parnes said.

"In a good way, for once," added Ms. Orlean, who had brown bangs and loved to deliver short sarcastic quips.

Ms. B was aware of the improvement in Zach's behavior. He wasn't acting quite as squirrelly or remote as before. But she hadn't said anything to anyone. She'd been waiting for someone else to notice. And now they had.

The truth was, Caleb had expected to lose again today. Luckily, Nathan finished the deciding round with a spectacular triple kill. But what truly surprised Caleb was something that he doubted anyone else on the squad had noticed: Zach had set that triple kill up for Nathan.

Now he and Zach were walking away from school. Leaving together after the eSports club had become a routine for them. It was a big change for Caleb, who usually felt he had to hurry home to do homework and chores. But he was glad not to be taking the late bus. For the past month, Crosby had gone out of his way to give Caleb the evil eye. *Is it just because we're on opposing squads? Or is it something more?* Caleb wondered.

Crosby's animosity seemed out of proportion, especially since, until today, his squad had won all their matches. The only other explanation for Crosby's hostility was that somehow he had figured out that Caleb was one of the two people who'd told Ms. B about his plan to cheat on the geometry test. But how? The only person Caleb told was Ms. B. And she had no reason to tell Crosby, right?

Anyway, Caleb had to admit that it was no fun being the target of Crosby's glares and sneers. Lately, every time Caleb saw Crosby, he felt tense and wary. It was hard for Caleb to imagine what it must have been like for Zach, who'd been going through that kind of torment from guys like Crosby for years.

But as he and Zach walked away from school, Caleb had other things on his mind. "That last round today?" he said. "The one we needed for the win? How'd you know Gavin's squad was working their way back through the spawn?"

"After nearly forty rounds against those guys you kind of know the way they think," Zach said.

"And when they came up the stairs at the end, you stepped out right in front of them," Caleb said. "You knew they'd see you. You made yourself a target so they wouldn't notice Nathan."

"I was super low on HPs," Zach said.

Caleb eyed Zach. "But how'd you know Nathan would get a triple kill?"

"I knew it was a possibility," Zach said. "He had the bazooka as his alternate weapon."

Caleb nearly stopped in his tracks. "You keep track of everyone's full load out?"

Zach quietly nodded.

He knew Nathan had the necessary firepower for the triple kill, and he sacrificed himself to give him the shot, Caleb thought. That was definitely something a lot of other gamers wouldn't do. Nathan would never sacrifice himself. He was too focused on racking up kills. Even more interesting to Caleb was that Zach seemed to know so much about what was going on in the game, and yet he went out of his way *to hide* his skills. It was like Zach became a different person during a match. Who could have guessed that there was this whole other side to him?

Just as he had every other time they walked home after a match, Zach stopped by the old stone wall and dropped his skateboard to the road. "See ya tomorrow," he said to Caleb, and then pushed off. Caleb wondered why Zach never let him go farther than that spot. What else was he hiding?

"See?" Mrs. Crane said with a big "I'm so proud of you" smile after Nathan told her how he sealed the Allied win that afternoon with a rare triple kill. He also told her that he was the best gamer on the squad.

"Always knew all those hours playing video games would pay off," Nathan teased.

His mother's proud smile slowly turned into a smirk.

"That's right, Mom," Nathan said. "The thing you always complained I did too much of is the thing I finally like about that stupid school."

Not that enjoying the eSports club was enough to let Nathan forgive his mom for forcing him to leave his friends and move halfway across the country to this two-stoplight dump of a town. Back when they first moved, he loved how his mother kept saying, "Don't worry, Nate, you'll make new friends." *Yeah, right! Like making friends is the easiest thing in the world.* "Just smile and introduce yourself," she said. *Sure, Mom,* he thought. *Introduce himself to who? Know who wants to be your friend when you're a new kid at school? Losers, that's who.*

His mother didn't understand that it wasn't only about making new friends. It was about having to reestablish himself. He hadn't lost just his old friends when he and his mom moved to Ironville. He'd lost his place, his position. He'd been popular at his old school. A winner. Someone who got invited to do stuff. Someone kids wanted to sit with at lunch.

Now he had to begin all over again. He'd even had to start

playing a new video game. For the past month he'd grinded *TGW* each night. It finally paid off today with that triple kill and his squad's win.

But as far as Nathan was concerned, this was just the first step toward a much bigger goal. The problem with the eSports club was that there was no one in it he really wanted to be friends with. Caleb seemed pretty smart, but he was too buttoned-up and goody-two-shoes for Nathan's taste. The captain of the squad, Emma, was okay, but outside of the club she could be really quiet and withdrawn. . . . Definitely not one of the popular kids. And the weird guy, Zach? Nathan had canceled him the second he'd laid eyes on him.

As far as the kids on the other squad, Crosby was just a clinger-on to Gavin, who struck Nathan as the last guy you'd want to meet in a dark alley. Tyler was too much of a joker to be able to tolerate for long. And that left Mackenzie, who was both stylish and mean enough to be popular but somehow didn't appear to connect with the girls Nathan had identified as the red-hot core of the seventh-grade social scene. Girls like Bethany Willis and Tanisha Proctor, who Nathan knew only by sight for now but who he would have to get to know better if he ever hoped to get where he wanted to go. At best, the eSports club was only a start, and little more than the first tiny rung up a long, long ladder.

One of the things Emma both liked and disliked about herself was her need to know. In one way she was proud that whenever there was a question about something she didn't know, she felt compelled to look it up. But it could be annoying, too. Especially with questions to which there were no obvious answers. Like, where had life come from? And how did the universe begin? And why were some girls, like her, stuck with dry, thin, curly hair? And was there anything she could do to become less anxious and more self-assured and outgoing? Maybe the answer to the last question was: stop being such a nerd and always looking things up!

But tonight, Emma couldn't help herself. She was researching Nazis. Everybody knew the Nazis were bad. Everyone knew that Adolf Hitler had been their leader and that the Nazis had killed millions of Jewish people during World War II. But now that she was looking online, it was confusing. Every source had a different estimate. Had 11 million people been killed? Or 17 million or 21 million? If roughly 6 million of those killed were Jewish, who were the others? And why had *they* been killed?

She paused in her research when the rest of the squad got online to discuss that day's match. During the past month they'd had a follow-up discussion after each match, and Emma had begun to see a pattern. Zach was almost always silent. Nathan talked a lot, usually about how great he was and where his squad mates needed improvement. It could be annoying, but Nathan was their best shot, so they put up with him.

That night, Emma half listened while Nathan recounted in minute detail how he'd pulled off the triple kill. It became obvious to her that Caleb was only half listening, too, because in the middle of Nathan's self-congratulatory ramble, he texted her: *Zach set up that triple kill.*

Emma scowled. Why did Caleb think that? But, as usual, Caleb had already anticipated her question. He sent a follow-up text: *Long story, but the point is, Zach sees the whole picture. Gets inside the other squad's heads. Knows what they're going to do. I think he should be our squad tactician.*

Except for Emma being captain, this was the first time anyone on the squad discussed the idea of specific titles. Emma understood why Caleb was making the suggestion. She had seen evidence that Zach was often more aware of what was going on in a round than the rest of them. But she also doubted that Nathan would respond well to the idea of Zach providing them with strategies. And since she was the captain, shouldn't she be the one who decided if there should be a squad tactician? For a moment, Emma was tempted to say that if Caleb thought Zach should be the tactician, why didn't Caleb just replace her as captain and make the decision himself? But Emma quickly reminded herself that she liked being captain. All day at school, girls like Mackenzie lorded over girls like her. But for a few hours once a week in the eSports club, Emma could tear Mackenzie to pieces in *The Good War*. She didn't want anyone to take that away from her.

While Crosby waited for 88Rising to come online that evening, he thought back to the match his squad lost that day. He hadn't been surprised. Gavin let himself get killed off early. It was obvious that the big red-haired boy wasn't interested in the game. He'd been in a funk all day. At lunch, Tyler had plucked a French fry off Gavin's plate, and Gavin had punched him so hard in the arm that Tyler had tears in his eyes. But Tyler was a moron. He should have known that when Gavin was in one of his black moods, you kept your distance.

Seeing those tears in Tyler's eyes reminded Crosby of how lucky he was to be on Gavin's good side. It was a relief a month ago, when Crosby figured out how Ms. B knew about his plan to cheat on the geometry test. When Crosby awoke in the middle of the night, it was because he'd remembered who sat in front of him and Gavin on the bus most mornings. It was those two sixth graders who always shut up the second Gavin and Crosby sat down behind them. And who sat in front of the sixth graders? Extra Credit Caleb. Crosby knew he sometimes forgot to use his inside voice. And he recalled how the whole time he was telling Gavin about his plan to cheat, Caleb was gazing out the window with one ear aimed back toward them. So Caleb definitely could have overheard him. And it would be just like Caleb to snitch to Ms. B.

88Rising got online, interrupting Crosby's thoughts. "Hey, CrossBow."

"Hey, bro, you're late. What took you?" Crosby said.

"Got stuck talking to some wacko," 88Rising said. "You'll love this, CrossBow. The guy was telling me about this organization called the Illuminati that's plotting to take over the world. Guess where he says their secret headquarters are? Under the Denver airport."

"What?" Crosby asked with a laugh.

"Crazy, right?" 88Rising said. "I mean, that's the thing

about the internet. It's overrun with lunatic conspiracy theories. Lesson number one: You can't believe everything you hear."

"Right," Crosby agreed, although the truth was that he hadn't heard much one way or the other. "It makes you wonder what you can believe."

88Rising was quiet for a moment. Then he said, "You can believe what we've talked about, CrossBow. That America was founded as a white country for people of European heritage. I'm not saying that America needs to be a hundred percent white. I mean, I like Mexican food as much as the next guy. But I don't think you'll be able to say that America is America at the rate we're going. It's gotten so bad that you can't even say Merry Christmas anymore without people losing their minds. You told me you work in fulfillment, right?"

"Uh, yeah," Crosby said. He'd told 88Rising that he worked in an Amazon warehouse because that was what his dad had done before his parents had split up.

"Imagine what it would be like if all your coworkers were black and brown and yellow," 88Rising said. "Imagine if your boss was some brown guy wearing a freaking turban? Think you'd be comfortable in a situation like that?"

Crosby had no idea how he'd feel. He wasn't sure he'd ever seen anyone wearing a turban. But he could sense the answer 88Rising expected from him. "Guess not," he said.

"See? That's what I like about you, CrossBow," said 88Rising. "You're smart and you're honest. You tell it like you see it. With the liberals breathing down our necks, guys like you and me have to stick together."

Crosby straightened up in his chair and smiled. He liked hearing that.

"Hey, CrossBow, know what?" 88Rising said. "Maybe it's time we shared our real names. What do you say?"

Crosby was surprised. That was a big step. People didn't share their real names online unless they felt a strong bond with each other.

"I'm Dave," 88Rising said.

"I'm Crosby."

"Nice to know you, Crosby. Now what do you say we play some *TGW*?"

They played until Crosby's aunt Mary called him for dinner. Crosby went into the kitchen feeling good, like he'd just made a new friend. A real friend. His mom was sitting at the kitchen table wearing an old pink robe and a blue scarf on her head to cover up the hair loss caused by chemotherapy. She smiled weakly at him. She was thin and her skin was a sickly gray. Crosby felt his body tighten. He couldn't get used to seeing her like that. Every time he did, he had to fight back tears.

While Crosby's mother had always been slender and gentle, her sister, Crosby's aunt Mary, was short, stocky, and pushy. She was the sort of person who always had an opinion and let you know it. That evening, Aunt Mary served him a bowl of spaghetti and meat sauce. Crosby's mom's dinner was a bottle of chocolate Ensure and a handful of colorful pills. Crosby was an only child, and he hadn't seen his father in years. He wasn't even sure where his father was anymore. Sometimes Crosby woke in the middle of the night wondering what would happen if they got to the point where his mom could no longer live at home. What would happen to him? Where would he live?

They'd hardly begun to eat when Aunt Mary asked if he was still in the eSports club. Crosby knew that she was trying to be like a mother to him because his own mother was now often too weak to do it. But having never been a mother herself, Aunt Mary really stank at it.

"Yes, and for your information, there are girls in the club," Crosby said, because he had a feeling that was what she was going to ask next.

"Good," Aunt Mary said. "And what about when you're online here?"

"I don't know," Crosby said. "I just play with people."

"Do you know who they are?"

"Not usually," Crosby said. "It doesn't matter."

"Oh, I think it does," Aunt Mary said in that accusing tone of hers. Like no matter what he did, it was wrong. "I've read that there are all sorts of predators who use gaming as a way to meet boys. Has anyone ever asked you for a photo of yourself?"

"You must think I'm really stupid," Crosby snapped at her.

"Crosby, please," his mother said softly.

"Sorry, Mom." Crosby turned to his aunt. "No one's ever asked, and I'd never do it if they did."

"Do people say racist things?" Aunt Mary asked. "Or sexist?"

"Not really," Crosby said.

His aunt leaned forward. "Not really?"

Crosby knew he'd made a mistake. "I mean, no, never," he said, although that wasn't quite true.

"That's hard to believe, considering there's sexism all over the internet," Aunt Mary said to Crosby's mother. "Men assume that technology is their domain and a place where women can't be their equals. A place where they don't *want* women to be their equals." She turned to Crosby. "I assume you follow professional gaming teams. Are there any women gamers on them?"

"Some," Crosby said.

"A tiny minority," said Aunt Mary.

Crosby was so tired of her attitude. "I guess you'd say women should be on professional football teams, too?"

"No," said Aunt Mary. "They can't. Their physiologies are different. Men have larger skeletons and more muscle mass than women. And even among men, only about one in a thousand is exceptional enough to play professional football. But the reason there are so few women gamers isn't physical. It's because they don't see themselves on screens. Look at the hero in most video games and what do you see? A strong, white male with a fast car and a gorgeous girlfriend."

"What about Lara Croft, Zelda, Calamity," Crosby shot back.

"Let me guess. All skinny girls with big chests and pretty faces?" countered Aunt Mary.

"Please. I think we've argued enough about this tonight," Crosby's mother said wearily. Crosby leaned back in his seat. His eyes met Aunt Mary's and they instantly shared an understanding. If there was one thing they *could* agree on, it was that all this arguing wasn't doing his mother any good.

WEEK FIVE

GAVIN'S SQUAD: 3
EMMA'S SQUAD: 1

Caleb got on the bus to school feeling worried, stressed, and excited. He was worried because all week long the yearbook portrait photographer had been at school, and the guy seemed disorganized and scattered. Umbrella lights fell over in the middle of shoots. The photographer got the names of students mixed up. He tripped over power cords. Was Caleb's father right when he said cheaper didn't always mean better? Had Caleb made a mistake recommending him? That would really hurt his chances of becoming the yearbook's managing editor next year.

But Caleb was also excited because last night a reporter from the local Ironville TV station came to his house to interview him and his parents about the eSports club. And later today a crew would video the club in action. The story angle was about Caleb being only in seventh grade and having been the force behind the creation of the eSports club and the grant for the Providia computers.

Caleb reminded himself that ITV, which stood for Ironville

Television, reached only households in Ironville. But still, how many seventh graders had ever had a story done about them?

When Gavin and Crosby got on the bus a few stops later, they were wearing matching red T-shirts with short, jagged white lightning-bolt logos on the front. Caleb immediately wondered if the shirts had something to do with the match that afternoon. Crosby stopped in the aisle just past Caleb's seat and told the sixth graders who sat there to move. Caleb heard the kids quickly scoot from the seat and Gavin and Crosby slide in.

A moment later, Caleb felt Crosby's warm breath in his ear. He knew that Crosby was trying to scare him by getting that close. Caleb turned in his seat. Crosby's face was so close that Caleb could see the blackheads in his forehead.

"Know why I've been giving you the hairy eyeball for the past month?" Crosby asked. "Because I know it was you who told Ms. B about me cheating on the geometry test."

It took all of Caleb's willpower not to blink or look away. But there was no way Crosby could know that for sure. Caleb trusted Ms. B. She never would have told Crosby how she knew about his plan. Besides, Ms. B had said that someone else had also told her about it. Caleb decided that Crosby was bluffing. He'd said that just to see how Caleb would react.

"What are you talking about?" Caleb asked.

Crosby's eyes narrowed. He glanced at Gavin, then back at Caleb. "You better watch yourself."

"Last Friday in the hall three boys came up to me, very excited, and asked if it was true that the school had an eSports club," Ms. B told Principal Summers in the computer lab. "I almost asked where they'd been four weeks ago when we had the informational meeting."

Principal Summers sighed. "No matter what we do, it seems like half the kids don't listen to the morning announcements."

"So I told them, yes, there's a club," said Ms. B, "but right now we're just testing the idea to see what works and what doesn't. If it goes well, hopefully we'll be able to expand for the spring semester."

"Then there's growing interest?" Principal Summers asked.

"Which may grow even more after the ITV story comes out," Ms. B said, reminding the principal that the film crew would be coming to the eSports club that afternoon. "But here's what's interesting. It turned out that those boys weren't asking about the club because they want to play. They were asking because they want to add commentary and stream the matches on Twitch."

Principal Summers frowned. "Sorry?"

Ms. B might have been far from savvy when it came to internet gaming, but she knew about Twitch. She explained that the boys wanted to broadcast the matches online so that other kids could watch.

"Kids want to watch other kids play video games?" Principal Summers asked, puzzled.

"Just like any other sport," Ms. B said.

The principal's eyebrows dipped. She strolled along the

table where the Providia monitors sat. "Well, anything that gets the students involved is good," she said. "But what about the educational part? Are students using these computers for anything besides gaming?"

"Let me show you something." Ms. B sat down at one of the computers and pulled up an animation. "Remember those models of the solar system we used to make with papier-mâché and clothes hanger wire?"

"Oh yes." Principal Summers smiled at a memory. "What a mess."

"And also completely inaccurate," said Ms. B. "The solar system isn't just sitting there. It's moving through space at something like fifty thousand miles an hour." She swiveled the monitor so the principal could see an animation showing the sun moving in a straight line through space while the rest of the solar system corkscrewed around it. "This is what our solar system *really* looks like. The graphics cards in these Providias make projects like this possible. Our students could never have done this on our older computers."

"Students created this video?" Principal Summers asked, surprised.

"Yes," said Ms. B. "Not only are they learning computer programming, but they're applying what they learn to other disciplines. In this case, science."

Principal Summers smiled. "Promise me you'll mention that when the ITV people come this afternoon. It's something we'll want everyone to know."

"Rest assured," Ms. B said.

The first bell rang, and Ms. B headed to her classroom feeling jubilant. Not only was interest in the eSports club growing, and not only would the ITV crew be interviewing her as the club's faculty advisor that afternoon, but she'd also just proved how useful the new computers were educationally.

Alas, her jubilation was fleeting. Moments later, when she entered her classroom, she saw something that gave her pause. Gavin and Crosby were wearing matching red T-shirts with white lightning-bolt logos. What was that about?

In the hall after second period, Emma found herself stuck behind Gavin and his goon squad as they marched shoulder to shoulder like linemen on the football team. They were all wearing red T-shirts. Mackenzie, who was the second-tallest after Gavin, fit right in. Only, she'd added a gold chain to her outfit. Tromping down the hall, Gavin's squad seemed to enjoy making everyone go around them.

Tyler pointed when they passed the custodian's closet. "Ah, vas ist das?" He asked in a loud imitation of a German accent.

"Das ist dah broom room, mein freund," answered Crosby.

"Jawohl," said Tyler. The goons chortled appreciatively. Just then, Tyler looked back over his shoulder and saw Emma following them. He gave Crosby a nudge.

Crosby and the others stopped. They were like a human wall blocking Emma from going any farther. They crowded in so close that she could have reached out and touched them. A tremor of nervousness rippled through her.

"Prepare to be annihilated today, Allied vimp," Crosby said in his stupid German accent. "From now on vee vant to be zee Axis full-time. Instead of switching back and forth."

"Jawohl, no one can withstand the Axis might," Tyler chimed in.

"And den vee can keep track of our vins und losses for zee whole season," Crosby added.

It was hard for Emma to process what they were saying when they were so close and looming over her like a bunch of real-life *Mario Bros.* Koopas. She knew this was a form of bullying. But would they dare do something to her right there in the crowded hall? Pick on a girl who was literally half Gavin's size? She didn't know what came over her, but she straightened up and demanded firmly, "Would you all, like, take a giant step back?"

For an instant, the goon squad was still. Crosby and his friends looked astonished that Emma had raised her voice at them. Now Emma felt anxious. She didn't know what to expect. Would they laugh and ignore her demand? Or crowd in even closer? But they did neither. Instead, Gavin took a step back. And when he did, Crosby and the rest followed.

"So, uh, what do you think about having permanent sides?" Crosby asked without his previous bluster.

"I'll ask my squad what they think," Emma replied.

"I thought *you* were the captain," Mackenzie needled. "Why can't you just decide yourself?"

"That's not the way we do it on our squad," Emma answered, trying to stand tall—well, as tall as someone who was five foot two could stand—and looking Mackenzie straight in the eye.

It was raining, so they stayed inside for gym. Ms. Patrick had them all sit on the floor. She was dressed in a blue tracksuit, a whistle hanging around her neck.

"I hear that money is going missing from gym lockers," she said. "How many times do I have to remind you to lock your lockers after you change into your gym clothes? That's why they're called lockers, folks. Because you're supposed to *lock* them. Now choose captains for capture the flag."

There were four captains in capture the flag, and Caleb was one of them. For as long as he could remember, whenever kids chose up teams, Zach was always among the last to be picked. It didn't matter that he was agile and fast. No one wanted him. It was true that sometimes Zach spaced out and appeared to forget what was going on. But as soon as Ms. Patrick called him out, he'd get right back into whatever game they were playing.

So today, instead of letting Zach be one of the last chosen, Caleb made him one of the first. To his surprise, Zach winced unhappily. Caleb was perplexed. He thought getting picked early would make Zach feel good. Why was the kid acting like he wished he had not been picked at all?

Some girls didn't like gym because they got sweaty or it messed up their hair and makeup. Emma didn't care about that, but she did care about being compared to her sister, Sarah, who was six years older. Sarah was now a freshman at college on a soccer scholarship, but she could have excelled at any sport. As a result, Emma had spent most of her school career being compared to her remarkable sister, and not always in a good way.

And Emma had a particular dislike for capture the flag. It was a game in which punchers, trippers, and shovers were on the loose, and Ms. Patrick's eyes couldn't be everywhere at once. Emma had seen kids hurt others when the gym teacher wasn't looking. She anxiously scanned the players, trying to spot the ones she'd need to avoid. Fortunately, Mackenzie, who almost always found an excuse for not dressing for gym, was one of half a dozen kids sitting in the bleachers still wearing their school clothes. So that at least was good news.

The game started, and everyone raced around trying to steal flags. While the quick, athletic kids tried to dodge their way to the flags, others hung back, waiting for an opening to sneak in. Or, if they were like Emma, they only pretended to wait for an opening, while they really waited for the period to end.

Suddenly, Ms. Patrick blew her whistle. A girl named Carrie was sitting on the gym floor, clutching her knee, tears running down her face. Ms. Patrick told someone to get a cold pack from her office and then squatted beside the girl, offering her comfort. It seemed like the whole class was watching, but when Emma glanced away, she saw Crosby and Tyler backing Zach against a wall.

Nathan waited for his mother to pick him up after school. He knew he should have been happy. Emma's squad won again, and for the second week in a row he'd had a massive kill streak. And a local TV crew was there to record the match, so that meant he was going to be on TV! Plus the whole match had been streamed live on Twitch. Anyone who watched it had seen how well he'd played.

But Nathan wasn't happy. Even though he was clearly the star player on Emma's Allied squad, the TV crew's camera had focused mostly on Caleb. And it galled Nathan that Emma had made Zach the squad tactician. *Why do we need a tactician?* he wondered. All they needed to do was keep playing better than Gavin's Axis squad. And something else bothered Nathan. Anyone who watched ITV was going to see him sitting next to Zach the Wack. A guy like Caleb, who everyone already knew, didn't have to worry if people saw him sitting next to a weirdo like Zach. But most kids at Ironville Middle School still didn't know Nathan. So if they saw him with Zach, they were liable to label Nathan a wack by association.

Does that sound cruel? Nathan thought. *Well, sorry. It's just the plain truth.*

"Hey," someone said.

Nathan turned. Two kids were coming toward him.

"Good game," one said.

"You had some awesome headshots," said the other.

"You watched the stream?" Nathan asked, surprised.

"Yeah," said the first. "Magic: The Gathering ended early. Our friend Alex was doing the cast for your match, so we watched."

"It was cool," the second kid chimed in. "You're, like, the kill."

A car pulled up, and the two kids got in. As Nathan watched the car turn toward the school exit he felt a lot better. He was the Kill Streak King!

○

Walking from school after the match, Zach pretended to be a caster: "Caleb 'Xtra Cred' Arnett has suddenly become the multimillionaire face of *The Good War*, the impossibly popular boots-on-the-ground World War II video game with more than 100 million active players every day. A former star gamer on the Allied squad at Ironville Middle School's eSports club, Xtra Cred's parents recently let him drop out of school to grind *TGW* for ten hours a day while interacting with fans who pay to watch him play."

He and Caleb were feeling giddy after their squad's second straight win over Gavin's squad.

"Xtra Cred also competes in tournaments around the world and has numerous endorsement deals," Caleb added.

"Right!" Zach cried. "Xtra Cred's reach is staggering. More than twelve million followers on Twitch, almost twenty million on Instagram, and nearly four million on Twitter."

"He's been featured on the cover of *ESPN The Magazine*. Wherever he goes, he is mobbed by adoring fans," Caleb added. "Rumor has it that Nike will name its newest eSports shoe the Xtra."

"Xtra Cred for Nike!" Zach guffawed. "The complete clothing line."

"The gaming jacket," Caleb suggested.

"The athletic briefs!"

They both cracked up.

When they got to the old stone wall, Zach didn't want Caleb to leave. They'd had so much fun pretending to be casters. Part of Zach wished they could keep going, all the way back to his place. But another part of him was uncertain. It was true that Caleb had been nicer to him for the past month than practically any kid Zach had ever known. Not only had Caleb picked Zach first for capture the flag today, but when Tyler and Ratface Crosby had ganged up on him, Caleb had come over and told them to lay off.

But it was still hard for Zach to accept Caleb as a true friend. He'd had too many bad experiences. As a result, Zach had learned to be extra careful.

The boys stood beside the stone wall without speaking for a few moments. Then Caleb said, "Sorry about what happened in gym today. Tyler and Crosby are total jerks."

Zach shrugged. It wasn't that he'd gotten used to being picked on. Getting picked on was something no one ever got used to. But he had gotten to the point where it was just another burden like vaccinations and the dentist, another fact of life, and something he preferred not to be reminded of. Zach changed the subject. "What's it like having them do a TV show about you?"

"Not just me," Caleb said. "About the eSports club."

"But they spent a lot of time talking to you," Zach said.

"Guess we'll see when it's on TV," Caleb said. Then he glanced off in the direction he usually went when they parted. Zach didn't want Caleb to go, but he figured the kid probably had other things to do. But then Caleb said, "I saw what you did today in the last round. With the smoke grenades."

Zach was surprised and pleased. He hadn't been sure anyone had noticed. "Yeah, after last week, I figured we needed to do something a little different."

"Control the ground," Caleb said.

"When Gavin's squad watches the match tonight, they'll figure it out," Zach said. "So we'll need to come up with something else for next week."

Caleb studied him for a moment. Feeling Caleb's eyes on him made Zach nervous. He began to blink and fidget.

"You really think about this stuff a lot, don't you?" Caleb said.

Zach stared at the ground. "That's what makes it fun, right?"

"Especially when you beat jerks like Gavin and Crosby," Caleb said.

Zach grinned. He and Caleb shared a fist bump. And he made a decision.

◡

"No way," Caleb muttered in disbelief. Zach's bedroom was a shrine to skateboarding, surfing, and gaming. Three skateboards were lined up in a wooden rack. Helmets on pegs jutted from the wall. On a small desk sat side-by-side monitors. Posters of surfers and skaters hung on the walls.

Almost everything in the small room had a homemade feel. The desk looked like it was once part of a door. The bookcase was built out of mismatched pieces of plywood. Even the skateboards looked like they'd been constructed by hand.

Caleb had never been in a trailer home before. Truth was, he didn't even know there was a trailer park in Ironville. He could tell that Zach was nervous about him being there. The kid was blinking fast, one finger under his hair digging at his scalp, clearing his throat loudly over and over. Caleb had learned that getting Zach to talk helped calm him down. His eyes traveled to the ceiling, where an honest-to-God surfboard hung in an overhead rack with a rope attached to a pulley.

"You surf?" he asked.

Zach shook his head. "Found it in someone's garbage. But maybe someday."

Caleb reached up and touched the rack holding the board. "How's it work?"

Zach untied the pulley rope from a cleat and let the rope slide through his fingers. The rack slowly dropped until it was waist high. Now Caleb could see why the board had been thrown out. One of the fins was broken, and the fiberglass deck was cracked and peeling away from the foam underneath. Zach pulled the rope, and the rack rose back up to the ceiling. The design was both homemade and ingenious.

"A month ago, I would have asked who made this rack," Caleb said. "But now I'm pretty sure I know."

Zach stopped blinking and smiled. Strangely, now it was Caleb who felt stressed. He turned to the homemade bookcase stuffed with paperback books. The paperbacks were old, with cracked spines and tattered covers. Caleb checked the titles: *Snow Crash, Neuromancer, Feed, Ready Player One, Do Androids Dream of Electric Sheep?* He'd never heard of any of them. Nor did he recognize them as required reading for school.

"You read for fun?" he asked.

Zach nodded. "Mostly cyberpunk. I get 'em used."

Caleb pulled *Do Androids Dream of Electric Sheep?* off the shelf and flipped through the stiff yellowed pages. "I would have figured you for ebooks," he said. He expected Zach to say that he liked real books because his eyes needed a rest from screens. Or that ebooks were too expensive. But Zach said, "I like to look at them. Sometimes I don't even take them off the shelf. I just look at the spines and daydream about a scene I really liked. Know the movie *Blade Runner?*"

Caleb nodded. He'd heard of it.

"It's kind of based on the book you're holding," Zach said. "Philip K. Dick is probably my favorite author."

Caleb slid the book back onto the shelf. How many kids had a favorite author? Did he know *any?* What he did know was that most kids had an act, a front, a face they put on for the rest of the world to see. One was a tough guy. Another wanted to be everyone's friend. In language arts, Mr. Parnes once read them a quote from Shakespeare: "All the world's a stage, and all the men and women merely players."

Deep down, Caleb knew that was true of him. He spent most of his time trying to act like the person he thought he should be. But Zach was different. Once he got to know you, a lot of the weird stuff faded and the real Zach started to show through. The kid who really knew what was going on when they played *TGW*. The kid who gave himself up for his squad. And this room, with its skateboards, surfboard, and books. It all felt sincere and authentic. It wasn't for extra credit. Zach wasn't trying to impress anyone. This was who he was.

Zach gestured to the rack of skateboards. "You ride?"

Caleb shrugged. "Tried it a few times."

A smile crept across Zach's lips. He pulled a couple of boards from the skateboard rack. "Grab a helmet. Let's go."

Emma assumed that she was going to hate being streamed. The idea of other kids watching her play, seeing her make mistakes, unnerved her. To make matters worse, the casters had set up a camera in the computer lab to show the players in real time. So that afternoon, Emma played very cautiously, afraid to do anything wrong. But after the first round, she heard Zach's voice in her headset: "Just go for it, Emma. Don't hold back."

At first, Emma was startled that Zach noticed the way she was playing. But then she remembered what Caleb said about Zach knowing almost everything that happened during a match. Most players were so busy trying to improve their KD ratios that they didn't pay attention to what their teammates were doing. But Zach was different.

Emma began to play more aggressively. And in the end, she did fine and contributed to their win. And the funny thing was, for once she didn't have to worry about being compared to her perfect older sister. Because Sarah had never been into gaming.

It was still early evening and Emma had finished her homework. There were other things to do—YouTube, Netflix—but instead she turned to Google. A week ago, on her own, she'd begun to read about the Nazis and the millions of people they'd killed during World War II. Now she read that Adolf Hitler believed that the Jewish people were an inferior race and a threat to German racial purity. Hitler believed in the superiority of the Germanic peoples, whom he called the Aryan "master race." For Hitler, the ideal "Aryan" was blond, blue-eyed, and tall. This seemed ironic, since Hitler himself was short and had very dark hair. And yet, he'd insisted that the German race had to remain pure in order to one day take over the world.

Emma's phone vibrated. That was strange. She hardly ever got a notification. She went to Instagram . . . and froze. It was a photo someone had taken at that afternoon's match of her looking dreamily at Caleb between rounds. They'd made Emma look like a dog with her tongue hanging out. The caption read: *Oh, Caleb, you are my master.*

Crosby drummed his fingers impatiently while he waited for his computer to boot up. It sucked that the Axis squad lost again today, but he reminded himself that it was just a dumb middle school club. And speaking of middle school, what annoyed him even more than losing the match was what happened in gym during capture the flag. He and Tyler had Zach the Wack cornered while Ms. Patrick was distracted helping some girl who'd hurt her knee. They were about to have a little fun when Extra Credit Caleb got involved. The next thing Crosby knew, Ms. Patrick blew her whistle and ordered him and Tyler to go to her office and wait for her.

Would she have noticed what they were doing if it hadn't been for Caleb? Why couldn't that jerk mind his own business?

Later in her office, Ms. Patrick chewed out him and Tyler for picking on Zach.

"We didn't mean anything by it," Crosby had said. "We were just having some fun."

"We weren't going to hurt him or nothing," Tyler said.

"How many times do you have to be told that you don't have to hurt someone to bully them?" Ms. Patrick asked irately. "Intimidation is a form of bullying. Ganging up on someone is a form of bullying."

The period was ending, and Ms. Patrick had to go back out to the gym. She let Crosby and Tyler off with a warning that if it happened again, she'd send them straight to the principal's office.

Later, at lunch, Crosby told Gavin what had happened. "That's twice that Extra Credit has ratted on me. He told Ms. B about me cheating on the geometry test. And now this thing in gym. I swear, bro, the time's come to do something about him."

Gavin unwrapped a piece of brown candy and popped it into his mouth. He didn't say anything, but Crosby had to believe he agreed.

Now, at home, Crosby's computer finally booted up. He was glad to see that Dave was online. He'd been out of touch for the past few days, and Crosby had gotten worried. Had he said something that had ticked Dave off? Talking to Dave made him feel good. It made him feel like he was part of something. Dave listened and respected him. Not like his aunt Mary and Ms. Patrick and those other soy-milk-drinking feminazis with their stupid politically correct ideas.

"Hey, Dave," Crosby said.

"Hey, Croz," Dave said. This was new. Dave was giving him a nickname. Crosby immediately liked it. Giving each other nicknames was exactly what good friends did. They started talking, and Crosby forgot about losing that day's eSports match, and about Caleb the snitch.

"Where you been, bro?" Crosby asked.

"Gun show," Dave said. "Picked up an Anderson AM-15 and a double-drum magazine. You throw a rifle stock and moly steel barrel on it, and you got yourself one hell of a cannon. And the whole thing's as legal as the day is long. What do you carry, Croz?"

Crosby's mind went blank for a second. "Uh, a Bren."

Dave laughed. "I'm not talking about a video game gun. I meant your day-to-day piece, bro."

"Oh, uh, a Glock." Now Crosby managed to remember a name.

"Right. Old reliable," Dave said. Their connection went quiet for a moment. "How old did you say you were, Croz?"

"Nineteen."

"Where'd you get the Glock?"

"Gun store," Crosby said.

Once again Dave was quiet. Crosby wondered if he'd said something wrong. Did they not make Glocks anymore?

"Well, you know what they say," Dave finally said. "Use it in good health." He chuckled as if that was a joke, so Crosby chuckled, too. "But seriously, on a fundamental level," Dave went on. "It's all part of the struggle, Croz. Not just the right to bear arms, but the right to maintain our personal and religious identities, okay? The right to preserve our country as the forefathers intended. For too long the snowflakes have been taking it away. I mean, right now, Croz. Right under our noses. It's everywhere you look: gay marriage, abortion, Muslims in Congress. At some point you gotta take a stand. 'Cause if you don't, what's next? Know what I mean?"

Crosby thought he did. *Well, maybe.*

"I need to know that we can depend on you when that time comes, Croz," Dave said.

"Definitely," Crosby said, though once again he wasn't sure what Dave meant.

"Good to know," Dave said.

After that they played *TGW* until Dave said he had to go. As soon as he signed off, Crosby googled the age requirements for purchasing guns. It turned out you couldn't legally buy a pistol in a store until you were twenty-one. That made him feel stupid because Dave had known he was lying about the Glock. The funny thing was, if Crosby had said he'd bought a semiautomatic AR-15 type of assault rifle, that would have been fine. Because the age requirement on those was eighteen. But maybe being caught in that lie wasn't so bad. Crosby could still pretend he was nineteen. More importantly, even after Dave had caught him, he'd had important things to say. Dave still wanted to know that he could depend on Crosby.

As far as Crosby was concerned, he could definitely be depended on.

○

"Why were you at school so late?" Caleb's mom asked while she drove home. The sun was an orange ball just above the treetops.

"Had to make a deadline for the yearbook," Caleb lied. The truth was Zach had given him a skateboarding lesson. It was a little confusing at first because Zach rode Goofy Foot, while Caleb rode regular. Zach taught him the proper way to push off and ride, and the next thing Caleb knew, he was gliding along the asphalt. It was amazing! Almost like freedom from gravity. He hadn't wanted to stop, but he knew he had to walk back to school so that his mom could pick him up.

"Did you make the deadline?" his mom asked in the car.

Caleb said he had. He didn't like lying to her, but if he always lived the way she wanted him to, it wouldn't be much of a life.

"Did ITV come to school?" his mom asked next.

"Sure did," Caleb said. "They asked a lot of questions, but I guess we'll have to wait to see what they use on the show."

"Don't forget to send it to Grammy," Mrs. Arnett said. ITV only broadcast to a few thousand people around Ironville, but once the grandparents got hold of it, you could count on repeat screenings in retirement communities from Florida to Arizona. "Did they say when it would be on TV?"

"In a couple of days," Caleb said, and gazed out the window as they passed the old steel mill. These days it was a dark empty brick husk behind a rusty fence. Both of his grandfathers had worked there, and so had some of his uncles. After the mill shut down it was said that life in Ironville changed. People began to move away, and those who stayed had trouble finding steady jobs. It made Caleb feel proud that he'd gotten those Providia computers for the school. It wasn't the same as getting extra credit just for himself. It was something that benefited others. Something that Caleb was just starting to discover felt good.

WEEK SIX

THE AXIS: 3

THE ALLIES: 2

For the first time since the football team had been disbanded, Ms. B could feel excitement in the air. It might not have reached the level of rah-rah school spirit on the day of a big game, but there was a definite stirring in the halls. The match a week ago had been streamed. A few days later ITV began running the segment about Caleb and her and the eSports club. Her students were excited to see her on TV and she'd overheard kids in the hallways talking about how they hoped to join the club in the spring.

Not everything went smoothly. "I've gotten two calls from parents complaining about those red T-shirts Gavin's squad wore," Mr. Parnes said in the teachers' room at lunch the day after the ITV segment ran. "They said it reminded them of the symbol of the SS."

Ms. B felt a chill. Mr. Parnes was right. The SS had been an elite, and savage, unit of the Nazi party during World War II. Their symbol had been two white lightning bolts.

"And has anyone noticed that they've been talking with

German accents?" asked Ms. Dean, who taught math and was the yearbook advisor.

"They're playing a World War Two game between the Axis and the Allied forces," Ms. B explained. "Gavin's team is the Axis. But I should have recognized the lightning bolt sooner."

Mr. Parnes took off his glasses and cleaned them on the cuff of his plaid shirt. "Do you think maybe they're taking it a little too seriously?"

"I'm not sure I have a problem with it," said Ms. Orlean, the social studies teacher. "If the game were called *The Revolutionary War*, and Gavin and his friends wore red coats and pretended to have British accents, would that be any different?"

Mr. Parnes tapped his long, bony fingers against the tabletop. "I don't recall reading anywhere that the British were in favor of genocide."

After lunch, Ms. B found Principal Summers in the hall. They discussed the situation and agreed that the Axis team shouldn't wear the T-shirts again. Later, Ms. B spoke to Gavin, who looked completely surprised to learn what the lightning bolt represented.

"Believe me, Ms. B," he said. "I've got nothing against Jewish people. I don't even know any."

He assured her that he would pass the message to the other members of the Axis squad. Ms. B thought that settled the matter, but over the next few days, as the eSports club segment continued to be shown on ITV, she received emails from parents complaining about the T-shirts and questioning the idea of eSports at school. Ms. B answered each one, apologizing for the tees and reminding the parents that the computers and high-speed internet had been provided for free and were being used for academics as well as gaming. Gradually, the emails stopped. But several weeks later when it all went horribly bad, Ms. B would look back at those emails as the first inkling that what they were involved in wasn't just a game.

The day after the image of her as Caleb's pet appeared on Instagram, Emma stayed home from school. A stomachache had merely been a convenient excuse in the morning, but by noon, it was as real as each tortured breath she took. As real as each new comment added to the post. "Lapdog." "Freak." "Loser." "They should hold hands and jump off a bridge."

Her phone was the source of all her agony and despair, and yet she couldn't stop looking. Couldn't stop checking to see if any more awful comments had been added. It was torture.

By late afternoon the cyber spears and arrows had stopped flying. The hunters and haters had moved on to fresher targets. Going back to school the next morning was one of the hardest things Emma felt she'd ever done, but no one glowered. No one pointed a finger. No one called her lapdog. Everyone seemed to have forgotten.

Several days later, Emma stood on the lunch line feeling a sense of relief. By now, the pet post was ancient history, a billion posts ago on everyone's feed. She didn't know if Caleb had seen it. If he had, he hadn't said anything. So the damage appeared to have passed and Emma was looking forward to the match that afternoon.

"Well, well, look who's here," a voice behind her said.

Emma felt a shiver. Her stomach grew queasy as she turned to find Mackenzie and Isabella. She would have bet anything that Mackenzie had been the one behind the horrible Instagram. Now she braced herself for the inevitable cruel, biting comment. She might have been a better gamer than Mackenzie, but in almost every other way, she still felt inferior. That was the way it had always been. It felt like that's how it would always be.

"Bet you love being on the same squad as your lover boy," Mackenzie said with a sneer. Today she was wearing a pink embroidered top and a gold name necklace.

For a moment, Emma felt tongue-tied. She was certain that Mackenzie expected her to deny it. The Mistress of Microaggressions was no doubt thirsting for the sort of vile argument she adored. But then inspiration struck. "I do," Emma answered, "but he's not my lover boy."

Mackenzie and Isabella both blinked with surprise.

"But you wish he was," said Isabella.

Again, Emma tried to think of the last thing they'd expect her to say. "It wouldn't be the worst thing in the world. Don't tell me you've never liked a boy."

Like matching androids, Mackenzie and Isabella let their mouths fall open. They gasped and cackled. "Oh, I can't wait to tell him!" Mackenzie cried.

Suddenly, Emma feared she'd made a mistake. She thought back to the pet post. She'd survived, but never wanted to go through anything like that again. Mustering what little courage she had left, she said, "What difference will it make if you do?"

"Then he'll know you like him," Isabella said.

Emma suspected Caleb already knew. And so, of course, did everyone who'd seen the pet post. "And? So?"

Like fish gasping for air on the surface of a pond, the girls' mouths moved, but no words came out. "You'll . . . It'll . . . ," Mackenzie stammered. "You'll be humiliated."

"If you say so," Emma replied, and shrugged as if she didn't care. The truth was, she did. But after the pet post, could they really humiliate her any more than they already had?

After last week's match, Nathan had felt really good. Those kids had called him the Kill Streak King, and the next morning at the bus stop some other kids had nodded reverently at him. They also must've watched the stream. They'd recognized him!

On the bus, it got even better. Nathan listened in while two kids sitting in front of him talked. "You watch the match yesterday?"

The other said, "What match?"

"On Twitch," said the first. "The eSports club."

"What eSports club?" asked the second.

"Where have you been?" the first asked. "They play *The Good War* after school." He glanced at Nathan. "You're in it, right?" Nathan said he was. Things couldn't have been going better.

But then the weekend came. On Friday afternoon after school Nathan had nothing to do. The rule in his house was that he was supposed to stay off the computer until after dinner. It was a warm sunny afternoon, and Nathan wished he had someone to hang out with. But the only kids he was friendly enough with to ask were his Allied squad mates. He could have tried Caleb, but the guy was always busy with after-school activities. Emma Lopez would have been Nathan's next choice. She seemed nice and smart, but Nathan knew that other girls made fun of her. So being seen with her might make him look bad.

And that left Zach the Wack. The truth was, Nathan had come to respect Zach's gaming abilities. He even thought their styles complemented each other. Zach had a way of leading the enemy right into Nathan's sights. It was like Zach did the work and let Nathan take the glory. But, of course, that was because no one quick scoped faster than Nathan. Without his shooting skills, Zach's strategy would have been useless.

But Zach was a weirdo and there was no way Nathan could allow himself to be seen with him. And that left no one for Nathan to hang out with. He knew what his mother would say. *Be patient.* Maybe she was right. Now that the matches were being streamed, more and more kids would see him and know he was a good gamer. He wouldn't just have friends soon, he'd have the *right* friends.

But until that happened, there wasn't much to do. Nathan turned on ITV. Once again, there on the TV screen was the eSports story, with Caleb sitting in a living room with his parents. Caleb was talking about why he'd decided to push for the eSports club and how, with Ms. B's help, he'd gotten the grant for the Providias and fast internet. Then the scene shifted to Ms. B in the computer lab talking about how the school was benefiting academically thanks to the new computers. Finally, they showed a clip of last week's match, with Caleb, Emma, and Zach staring at their monitors, each with one hand racing over a keyboard, the other hand on a mouse. The scene shifted to the Axis squad in their matching red T-shirts.

Even though the show wasn't over, Nathan flipped to another channel. He'd already seen the ITV story half a dozen times. It turned out that he hadn't had to worry about being seen sitting next to Zach. Why? Because there hadn't been a trace of Nathan during the entire segment.

Squad tactician Goofy Foot moves stealthily through the halls. Few know that he's the genius behind the recent string of Allied victories. They've seen him on ITV and streams, but they assume he is just another member of the Allied squad. Only today must Goofy Foot face his greatest challenge yet. Caleb "Xtra Credit" Arnett has bidden that Goofy Foot join the Allied squad . . . in the forbidden land of the cafeteria.

Except for lunchtime detentions, not since sixth grade had Zach voluntarily entered the cafeteria. But Caleb had suggested he give it a try, pointing out that if Zach didn't like it, he could always go back to having lunch in the library. Zach reluctantly agreed, then nervously waited out in the corridor until most of the kids settled at their tables and were busy eating and talking with their friends. He entered the cafeteria and walked straight to the table where Caleb and Emma were sitting.

Caleb and Emma welcomed him with smiles. Zach had

just started eating the bag lunch he'd brought from home when Nathan arrived with a tray. "So what's our strategy for today's match, Mr. Squad Tactician?" he asked in a taunting way.

Zach immediately shrank back and wished he hadn't accepted Caleb's invitation to join them in the cafeteria.

"Chill, Nathan," Emma said. "You don't have to be like that."

Nathan rolled his eyes to show his disdain for the idea of a squad tactician. But then he changed the subject. "I know the Axis squad isn't allowed to wear those red T-shirts anymore, but all the pro teams have matching uniforms and logos. You think we should, too?"

Seated beside Zach, Caleb put his elbows on the lunch table and propped his chin in his hands thoughtfully.

"It'll make us look more professional on the stream," Nathan went on. "I heard that last week there were kids from other schools watching."

Zach found that curious. Did Nathan think they were going to get famous by being in a middle school eSports club? Was Zach so sure they wouldn't?

The match that afternoon was closer than ever. The Allied squad barely managed to win. The Axis played better and was more organized than in previous weeks. After the match, Emma asked her squad to get together online that night to review what had happened.

But that would be later. Right now, Caleb was at Zach's house again. They were in Zach's "workshop," which was actually the carport next to the trailer. It was jammed with scrap wood and tools.

"Where'd you get all this stuff?" Caleb asked, gesturing at some of the larger woodworking machines.

"Bought some of it used," Zach said. "My uncle gave me the drill press and table saw when he got new ones. He's the one who taught me woodworking."

That explained the homemade skateboards and furniture in Zach's room. Caleb picked up a set of shiny screwdrivers. They didn't look used. "Even if you got some things for free, the rest of this must've cost a lot."

Zach spun the blade of the table saw with his fingertip. He started making nervous throat-clearing sounds and bit his lip. Suddenly he wouldn't look Caleb in the eye. By now Caleb had hung around with him long enough to know why.

"I won't tell anyone, I promise," he said.

Zach looked out at the woods surrounding the trailer. The leaves had begun to turn yellow and red. "Wager matches."

Wha . . . ? Caleb almost asked Zach if he was for real, but all the tools in this workshop were proof that he was. Kids played wager matches for ten or twenty bucks at a time. A good player could make a hundred in a night. But you had to be *really* good because you weren't playing against your friends, or even against kids your own age. You were playing against randoms, and if *they* were playing wager matches, it meant they were really, really good. But there was something else Caleb didn't get. "If you can make money that way, why build your own furniture and skateboards? Why not just buy them?"

Zach wrinkled his forehead as if he found the question puzzling. "Because I like building things."

That night Emma met with the rest of the Allied squad online.

"Would someone please tell me the point of reviewing a match we won?" Nathan grumbled sourly.

"We nearly lost," said Emma.

"But we didn't," Nathan argued. "I don't know about the rest of you, but I have better things to do."

Emma didn't appreciate Nathan's attitude, but she agreed to make the review as fast as possible. Besides, there was really only one thing she wanted the squad to see—that throughout the match, instead of holding his position, Nathan had gone off by himself and gotten into one shoot-out after another. When they reviewed the rounds, it became obvious that the Axis players had figured out how to use Nathan's lone-wolf approach against the Allied squad by laying traps and ambushes.

"We have to play more as a unit," Emma said.

"I agree," said Caleb. "A strategy can't work if we're not all following it."

Emma assumed that Nathan knew they were talking about him.

"Look," Nathan said, "we've won the last three matches. I don't see what the problem is."

That was when Zach, who rarely said anything during these reviews, spoke up. "We nearly lost today because they developed a counterstrategy. My guess is that they'll try it again next week and probably win if we don't play better."

"Who gave you a crystal ball?" Nathan snapped.

Emma was tempted to inform Nathan that if he wasn't always so wrapped up in his own performance, he might have noticed by now that Zach probably knew the game better than anyone. But just then something popped up in the chat room:

DROOF: Long live the Axis. Sieg Heil!

DROOF: Long live the Axis. Sieg Heil!

DROOF: Long live the Axis. Sieg Heil!

DROOF: Long live the Axis. Sieg Heil!

DROOF: Long live the Axis. Sieg Heil!

Emma had no idea who Droof was or how he had found their chat. And why had he written *that*? Actually, she'd heard those last two words before. She was almost certain they were German. "Anyone know what that means?"

Caleb googled it. "The Germans used it in World War Two. It means 'hail victory.'"

Now Emma remembered where she'd heard that phrase. In a movie called *Schindler's List*. The Nazis in the movie said it.

"What's the big deal?" Nathan asked impatiently. "Just kick him."

Emma kicked Droof out of the chat. But she was still bothered by what the troll had written. Why "Sieg Heil"? What did that have to do with their chat? She decided it was just some dumb random jerk thing, and hopefully they'd never hear from him again. But suddenly Droof was back.

DROOF: Arbeit macht frei

DROOF: Arbeit macht frei

DROOF: Arbeit macht frei

"Okay. Now ban him," Nathan said. "This is stupid."

While Emma banned the troll, Caleb googled "Arbeit macht frei."

"It's German for 'Work sets you free,'" he said.

"Great," Nathan said, still annoyed. "So, are we going to stop and look up everything some stupid troll writes?"

"Wait," Caleb said. "A picture popped up when I googled it." He posted the image. It was those words, *"Arbeit macht frei,"* only in the photo they were atop a metal gate. Behind the gate were some old brick buildings.

"So?" asked Nathan.

"It's the entrance to Auschwitz," Caleb said.

"What's that?" asked Nathan.

○

Is it weird that Nathan doesn't know what Auschwitz was? Zach wondered. Or was *he* weird because he *did* know? It wasn't like they'd studied it in school. Zach only knew because he'd read *The Man in the High Castle.* He told the squad that Auschwitz had been a concentration camp in Poland where more than a million people had been slaughtered. The vast majority were Jewish. The words *"Arbeit macht frei"* were supposed to make those who entered the concentration camp believe that if they worked hard, they would eventually be allowed to go free.

"But they didn't have a chance," he said. "They were barely

fed and worked nonstop until they were too weak or sick to work anymore. And then it was the gas."

"It's true," Emma said. "I read that creepo Hitler called it his Final Solution. Get rid of inferior races so the Aryan race would remain pure and rule the world. I mean, talk about sick."

"And you know, it wasn't only Jewish people," Zach said. "Millions of Russians and Slavs too."

"Yeah," Emma said, "and when they weren't making weapons and ammunition for the German army they had other jobs, like pulling teeth out of the dead because the Nazis wanted the gold in the fillings."

No one spoke. Zach assumed they were all picturing it. He wondered if it was weird that a meeting about gaming strategy had morphed into a discussion of the greatest wartime atrocity in modern history.

Finally Nathan said, "Wasn't that, like, a hundred years ago?"

"Closer to eighty," said Caleb.

"Same difference," said Nathan.

It was nearly two a.m. Crosby and Dave had been playing *TGW* for hours. Crosby was playing great. He'd racked up a ton of kills.

"Been a good night for you, Croz," Dave said.

"Totally," said Crosby. "Looks like Christmas came early this year."

"Careful," Dave said. "Remember what I told you. If it was

up to them, we wouldn't be allowed to say 'Merry Christmas' anymore."

Crosby recalled that Dave had said something about Christmas a few weeks before. "Why not?" he asked.

"Because Jews and Muslims don't celebrate Christmas," Dave said. "So the liberals say it's a trigger. I mean, forget that the majority of Americans are Christian. Now we're supposed to say 'Happy holidays.'"

Crosby tried to remember if he'd ever heard anyone in Ironville say "Happy holidays." He figured he must have, but he couldn't precisely recall. It was the kind of thing you probably weren't aware of unless someone like Dave pointed it out.

"You know who Obama was?" Dave asked. "That Muslim president we had? No joke. His middle name was Hussein. Same as Saddam Hussein, the joker we fought in Desert Storm. Obama definitely was a Muslim. You want proof? All eight years that he was president, he sent out cards at Christmas that didn't say 'Merry Christmas' on them."

Crosby had heard of President Obama, but didn't know he was a Muslim.

"You know there are parts of the country where you can't put a Christmas tree in a public place?" Dave continued. "Or a Santa Claus? Because they're triggers, too. Because they're going to hurt some snowflake's feelings. Anything like that happening where you are?"

Crosby said he was pretty sure that wasn't a problem in Ironville.

"Well, good," said Dave. "But keep your ears open. If you hear anything like that, let me know, okay?"

Crosby said he would. Dave signed off with his usual

RaHoWa 14/88. Crosby stood up, stretched, and yawned. It was at times like this when he thought that Ironville might not be such a bad place to live. Yeah, it sucked that the middle school had lost its football team, and that there were a few feminazis like his aunt Mary around. But the town was mostly white, and people could say "Merry Christmas" all they wanted, and nobody gave a hoot where you put a Christmas tree or plastic Santa. Based on what Dave was telling him, it sounded like the rest of the country was going down the toilet.

WEEK SEVEN

THE AXIS: 3
THE ALLIES: 3

"Caleb?" Mrs. Arnett called out, sounding perplexed.

Darn, Caleb thought. He'd almost gotten past the kitchen without being seen. "Sorry, Mom. Can't stop," he called back. "Gotta catch the bus."

"Come back here right now, young man," his father ordered in his "voice of authority" tone.

Caleb stepped into the kitchen where his parents were having their morning coffee. They stared at him with shocked expressions.

"Green streaks?" The worry lines in his mom's forehead deepened.

The truth was, they weren't exactly green. Nor were they actually "streaks." After hearing the night before that the Axis was planning to wear new outfits for today's match, the Allied squad had all agreed to dye a lock of hair olive green.

"It's just for the match," Caleb explained. "It washes out with shampoo."

"Olive colored because you're supposed to be the Allies?"

Mr. Arnett guessed. That caught Caleb by surprise. He could only assume that his parents had been working overtime on the Hovernet. He hadn't told them that Emma's squad was the Allies for the rest of the semester. They'd learned that somewhere else.

"Is the Axis side dyeing their hair?" his mother asked.

"We don't know," Caleb said. "We just heard last night that they were going to wear gray shirts."

"Gray?" Mr. Arnett's eyebrows rose above his black-framed glasses.

Caleb nodded. "The Axis colors."

Mr. Arnett shook his head. "No, the Japanese uniforms tended more toward brown, and the Italians, tan."

"Uh, okay," Caleb said. His dad taught history at Ironville Community College, so it was hard to argue.

"Then the Axis squad is dressing like Nazis," Mrs. Arnett surmised.

"No, not like Nazis," Caleb said. "Like the Wehrmacht, the German soldiers."

"And what exactly would the difference between them be?" his father asked.

"The Nazis were the ones who killed all those people in the concentration camps," Caleb said, repeating what he'd heard. "The Wehrmacht were just the German soldiers fighting the war."

Mr. Arnett frowned deeply. "That myth has been thoroughly disproved. Almost all World War Two historians agree that the Wehrmacht cooperated fully with the Nazis when it came to murdering Jews. As did many German civilians who informed on their Jewish neighbors."

From the looks on their faces, Caleb thought his parents were taking this way too seriously. "Let's not make a big deal about it," he said. "It's just a video game."

"With students who dress as Nazis," his mother added sourly.

Caleb knew better than to argue. "If I don't go right now I'm going to miss the bus," he said, and dashed out of the house. He was used to his parents examining everything he did under a microscope, but they were wrong about this. It was just a game being played in an eSports club that *he* was responsible for creating. A game being played on PCs *he'd* written a grant proposal for. And soon it wouldn't just be the people of Ironville who saw him on their TVs. It would be many, many more.

○

In the teachers' room, Ms. Patrick was telling the others that someone was going through the gym lockers and taking money. "I don't know what to do," she said. "I'm the only teacher there, and I can't be out in the gym and inside the locker room at the same time."

"I've heard it's happening with the hallway lockers, too," said Ms. Dean, the math teacher and yearbook advisor.

Everyone agreed to remind their students to lock their lockers. Ms. B had resumed eating her broccoli salad when Mr. Bostwick, who taught eighth-grade English, joined her. "I'm having my LT kids write first-person narratives," he said. "Half of them want to set theirs in *The Good War.* I thought they meant World War Two, but they're talking about a video game? Something from an after-school club you're advising?"

"LT" stood for "lower track." They were below-average students who showed little interest in school. Most were biding their time until they turned sixteen and could drop out.

"It's a video game set in World War Two," Ms. B explained.

Mr. Bostwick's forehead wrinkled. Ms. B reminded herself that he didn't use email and insisted that he didn't have a computer at home. She expected him to complain that a personal narrative based on a video game was completely unacceptable. Instead he said, "They're actually excited about the assignment. And these are kids who never get excited about anything academic."

"Then you're pleased?" Ms. B asked, surprised.

"Bewildered is more like it," Mr. Bostwick replied.

Once again, Nathan was annoyed with the Allied squad. It was true that they'd agreed with his idea of dyeing a lock of their hair olive green for that day's match. But Emma still insisted that they discuss strategy. It was so stupid. It felt like they spent more time talking than playing. And none of them would listen when he pointed out that as long as they were winning, they didn't need a strategy. But they were a squad, right? So Nathan held his tongue.

Emma went first: "We need to keep communicating. Give callouts. Let us know where we're getting shot from and by how many people. And where they're deploying smoke grenades.

And if you hear a sniper shot, don't keep it to yourself. Tell us where a drone jammer is if he kills you, and where they're spawning. We need to know right away if someone is flanking you. Don't wait until you *think* a squad mate needs to know. Just assume they always need to know."

"How am I going to hear anything with you guys constantly talking?" Nathan asked doubtfully.

"Just call out who and where," Caleb said. "Keep it brief. No extra chatting."

"And hold your angles," Emma added. "The only way to win consistently is with teamwork."

Nathan groaned inwardly. There was no point in reminding them yet again that they already *were* winning consistently. "Anything else?" he grumbled.

"Actually, there is," Emma said. "Thanks to Zach."

But at that moment, Nathan's phone buzzed with an Instagram message:

UnPlug2gether Sat 7 PM

@WillBet17 @CPtendo @ShaProctor05
Get pumped!

Nathan stared at his phone in disbelief. Bethany Willis, Callie Potendo, and Tanisha Proctor were the most popular girls in the grade.

"Hey," he said to the squad. "Anyone just get something on Instagram?"

No one else had. Nathan studied the message more closely

to make sure it wasn't fake. But everything about it appeared real. He felt a rush of excitement. *The popular girls know who I am! They invited me to a party!*

○

It was lunchtime, and Emma was at her locker when she saw Nathan talking to Tanisha Proctor. Tanisha was tall and shapely, and she wore beautiful clothes. All the boys were gaga over her. Of course, Tanisha knew that, and she usually laughed at them. Emma had heard that she had a boyfriend in high school!

Nathan had dyed all the hair on the top of his head olive green, not just one lock. He caught Emma's eye and called out, "Hey, Emma, come here."

Emma bristled. *What am I, his dog?* But she went. Tanisha gave her a friendly smile. Their lockers were close to each other's, and she and Tanisha had been in school together since forever. While Tanisha had never expressed an interest in being friendly with Emma outside of school, she was always nice.

"You see the Axis today?" Nathan asked when Emma joined them. "They're wearing gray shirts. With medals."

"Metals?" Emma repeated, not getting it.

"*Medals.* The things they give to heroes," Nathan continued as if she were a moron. It suddenly hit Emma that this was an act. She knew what a medal was. Nathan was just trying to impress Tanisha.

"Okay," Emma's eyes met his, and didn't waver.

"No, it's *not* okay," Nathan snapped, continuing with the act. "It's gonna make us look stupid. Kids'll be watching on Twitch. They're gonna see the Axis decked out in uniforms and medals and us with this stupid green stuff in our hair."

Apparently, Nathan had chosen to forget that the green dye was *his* idea. But Emma knew that if she reminded him of that, all she'd do was embarrass him in front of Tanisha. And as much as he deserved to be embarrassed, it was Emma's job to keep the squad unified. So she said, "Let's talk about it in the cafeteria."

"But—" Nathan began.

"I said, we'll talk about it at lunch," Emma repeated firmly.

The bell rang. Nathan made a face and left. Emma opened her locker and dumped some books inside. When she closed it, Tanisha was standing there. She winked at Emma and said, "You go, girl."

Emma felt herself flush. Had anyone ever said that to her before? She didn't think so.

To prepare for that afternoon's match, Emma asked the Allied squad to meet in the computer lab during activity period to practice. As Caleb walked down the hall toward the lab, he had a lot more than that day's match on his mind: Would this be the day he heard from Brooke Ford?

Brooke Ford was famous. She was a reporter for KFKN, the CBS affiliate station in Franklin, and you could see her practically every night on the six o'clock news. A few days ago, she'd called Caleb and said she'd seen the ITV story and wanted to do a report about him and the eSports club. But before she proposed the idea to her boss, she needed to know if Caleb was interested, and whether he thought his parents would grant KFKN permission to interview him. Caleb had assured her that his parents would be agreeable. Great, Brooke had said. She would speak to her boss and get back to Caleb soon. In the meantime, she suggested that Caleb not say anything to anyone about it. She didn't want a competing network to get a jump on her.

Brooke Ford! Network television! Every time Caleb thought about it, he felt giddy. KFKN reached *millions of viewers.* Being interviewed by Brooke Ford would be the biggest thing that had ever happened to him.

When he got to the computer lab, Emma and Zach were already there. Nathan hadn't shown up. Caleb made himself calm down and practice until the last bell. Soon the Axis squad filed into the lab. Each one of them had a black Iron Cross pinned to the left pocket of a long-sleeve gray shirt with epaulets. Tyler had even brought a toy model of a German soldier with a submachine gun that he placed on the table, aimed at the Allied side.

Now Caleb felt a little silly that all Emma's squad had done was dye a lock of their hair olive green. But he reminded himself that the match was about who were the best gamers, not what they wore.

Nathan finally showed up, and Ms. B followed a few moments later. When she saw what the Axis squad was wearing, she froze. "Stop casting," she ordered the casters. Caleb felt his insides tighten. She sounded really serious.

The casters turned off the camera, and Ms. B spoke to the Axis team. "Weren't those medals worn by the Nazis?"

"Actually, Ms. B, they're from way before World War Two," Crosby quickly replied. "They go all the way back to the Teutonic Knights of the Middle Ages."

"And they're on the pickup bumpers my dad got for off-roading," added Mackenzie.

It was obvious that the Axis squad had prepared for Ms. B's reaction to the medals. Mackenzie typed something on her computer and turned the monitor for the rest of the club to see. She'd found images of knights from the Middle Ages in white robes adorned with black crosses.

Ms. B's forehead was still wrinkled. Several long silent moments passed. Finally, she told the casters that they could comment on the day's match, but they were not to use the camera that showed the gamers. Then she said: "Go ahead with your match. But I'll have more to say when you're done."

○

Crosby was royally ticked off. For the fourth week in a row the Axis squad had lost to a suck-up, a mousy girl, a wack job, and maybe one half-decent gamer. After being ahead three matches to none a month ago, the Axis squad was now behind in the overall match standings, three to four. And what really hurt was that, even with the camera turned off, the gameplay had been streamed for all on Twitch to see what a bunch of noobs the Axis squad had played like. And now, instead of letting them go home, Ms. B was making them stay in the computer lab while the Allied squad was allowed to leave!

"I understand that Iron Crosses have been around for thousands of years," she told them. "And if you were just wearing the crosses without the gray shirts, maybe that would be okay. Or if you wore the gray shirts without the crosses. But wearing them together reminds me too much of the Nazis. I want to make sure you're clear about what these symbols represent and how hurtful they could be to some people. Do you understand what I'm saying?"

The Axis squad averted their eyes and nodded the way kids do when they know it's expected of them. Tyler played with his plastic German soldier. Mackenzie sat with her arms crossed tightly. Gavin stared at his lap. Crosby glanced at the clock on the wall. "Are you going to keep us past the late bus, Ms. B?" he asked.

Ms. B's face darkened. "This is far more important than whether or not you catch a bus, Crosby. Many, many people, especially those of Jewish descent, lost their families in Nazi concentration camps. I think you need to understand what the Iron Cross represents to them. Those medals might have been worn at other times in history, but they are still symbols of hate, anti-Semitism, and terrorism. They are a reminder that the Nazis slaughtered millions of innocent people just because of their religion and ethnicity. Those murders had nothing to do with trying to win World War Two. The Nazis killed children and women and old people who were no threat to them. It was genocide, plain and simple."

Ms. B's face was flushed. It was obvious that she was really upset. The Axis squad cast their eyes down, trying to appear remorseful. But Crosby had doubts. A few nights ago Dave had told him about the Jewish threat to the United States. Unlike Muslims and Mexicans, Jews were white and could go almost unnoticed. According to Dave, even though the Jews were a small minority, they controlled most of the politics and banking.

Ms. B kept talking, and the members of the Axis squad kept sneaking peeks at the clock. A rain shower was passing outside. It would be really mean of Ms. B to make them miss the late bus and have to walk home in the rain or call their parents for rides. Finally, Ms. B added insult to injury by assigning them extra homework. That night they would each have to write out the definition of genocide and give three examples of it from history.

"And there'll be no more logos, medals, or anything else that hints of the Germans in World War Two," she concluded.

The rain had been brief, and patches of blue appeared between the clouds. The late-afternoon sun had begun to dry the asphalt between the puddles in the parking lot. When Ms. B left the school, she saw Principal Summers ahead of her, carrying a brown satchel.

Ms. B jogged to catch up, then told the principal about the Axis squad's gray shirts and Iron Crosses. "Honestly, I think we need to have an assembly about hate symbols," she said. "I get the feeling that these kids have no idea what some of these things mean."

Maybe it was Ms. B's imagination, but at the mention of an assembly, Principal Summers went pale. "After what happened at the last one?" she asked.

"But this would be with a different presenter," Ms. B said. "I'm sure we can find someone younger. Someone the kids can relate to. Hopefully there'd be a PowerPoint or video to help hold their attention. And I don't think it will cost us anything. I think there must be organizations that do that kind of assembly for free."

Principal Summers pursed her lips pensively. "I understand your concern, but I'm worried about blowing this out of proportion. We're talking about only a handful of students, while an assembly will introduce hate symbols to the entire student body. Kids who may be completely unaware that these things even exist. And if you bring up racist symbols, don't you have to include nooses? And if you talk about nooses, you have to talk about lynchings. I'm not sure all our kids are mature enough for that. And with anti-Semitism, you're obviously going to have to introduce the Holocaust and the ovens. I mean, of course, our students will have to learn about these things, but don't you think it would be better to learn about them in the appropriate historical context? So yes, they should learn about lynchings when they study the post–Civil War period. And about the Holocaust when they study World War Two. But I'm worried that dropping hate symbols into their laps out of context will be confusing to them. And I'm especially concerned about how their parents might react."

"But if they're being exposed to hate symbols here in middle school, shouldn't we be educating them now?" Ms. B asked.

Principal Summers gazed up at the last few dark clouds

drifting across the sky. "Ms. B, you and I both know that kids today are exposed to so much more than we were at their age. The internet has changed everything. Here in school we can't possibly keep up with what they see on their phones and computer screens. We have to depend on their parents to pick up some of the slack."

"Then maybe it's the parents who need to see the assembly," Ms. B said. "I mean, I consider myself a politically aware adult, and yet I had no idea what 'RaHoWa' and '1488' meant."

"I've never even heard of them," Principal Summers said.

Ms. B explained that "RaHoWa" stood for "Racial Holy War," something white supremacists spoke of as a solution to the "problem" of minorities. The number 14 stood for the fourteen words that made up a popular white supremacist rallying cry: "We must secure the existence of our people and a future for white children." And 88 stood for "Heil Hitler" because "H" was the eighth letter of the alphabet.

"And those are just three," Ms. B said. "There are dozens and dozens more."

Principal Summers's face scrunched with frustration. "I don't have to tell you that one of the problems we face here in Ironville is low parental participation. We've tried programs for parents before, and the turnout is always minimal. The ones who come aren't the ones we need to reach, and the ones we need to reach don't come."

"So there's nothing we can do?" Ms. B asked, feeling vexed.

"No, we always do something," Principal Summers insisted. "If there's an incident involving hate speech or a hate symbol, we send a notice to the parents suggesting they speak to their children about it."

"But that's being reactive instead of proactive," Ms. B pointed out. "Instead of teaching them not to use hate symbols and language, you're waiting until they use them and then responding."

Principal Summers nodded sadly. "I know, and I'm sorry, Ms. B, but it's the best we can do."

Caleb and Zach stood at the crest of a long hilltop road, strapping on helmets and pulling on gloves. Caleb's stomach felt like it was filled with fluttering butterflies. "You sure it's dry enough?" he asked.

"See for yourself," Zach said. "There's hardly any wet spots."

Caleb looked down the road and saw mostly sun-dried asphalt. "Tell me again how I stop?" he asked.

Zach rolled his eyes in good-natured exasperation. "We've been over this, like, a thousand times. If you're not going too fast, you can foot brake."

"I take my foot off the board and drag it on the ground," Caleb said.

"Right. And if you're going too fast for that, use the glove-down slide."

"Uh . . . Maybe you could show me that again?" Caleb asked meekly.

Zach sighed. It was obvious that Caleb was stalling. They'd practiced foot braking and the glove-down slide for the past two weeks. Caleb knew how to do them; but he was just scared.

"Listen, we don't have to do this hill today," Zach said. "No one's going to know."

While he appreciated Zach's offer to let him get out of boarding the hill, Caleb always wanted to succeed, and this was a new challenge. Yes, he was super nervous, but he knew he'd be totally disappointed in himself if he didn't give it a shot.

"Just remember," Zach said. "If you do start to fall, make sure you tuck and roll."

Caleb recited what he was supposed to do. "Elbows bent, tuck, and try to roll over a shoulder." To demonstrate, he crouched down and pulled his elbows in.

"Right," Zach said. "The one thing you don't want is a hard stop. But you're not going to fall. You're going to control your speed by . . . ?"

"Carving!" Caleb answered. Last week Zach had shown him how to carve on a gradual slope. Carving was cool. Surfers carved. Snowboarders carved. And in a few moments, Caleb told himself, he, too, would carve.

"See you at the bottom." Zach pushed off and gracefully wove down the long tree-lined road until he disappeared around the bend far below.

Caleb was left alone at the top of the hill. *Now what?* he asked himself. His heart was thumping in his chest. He knew he had to get down the hill one way or another. If he walked, it would take forever and Zach would know that he'd chickened out. Caleb didn't want to think of himself as a wuss. Besides, he liked the idea of doing something purely for the sake of the thrill. Something that wasn't going to be graded. That didn't count for extra credit. Something that was *just for fun.* He wanted to lose himself in the exhilaration and adventure. When was the last time he'd done something solely because it was fun? Carving was fun. Caleb was willing to bet that going fast was fun. Well, going a little fast, at least.

He gazed down the hill again. It was a lot steeper and longer than the one he and Zach had practiced on. His heart was still thumping. *Maybe this isn't a good idea. . . .*

Oh, come on, you wuss. At least try. . . .

He pointed the board down the hill and pushed off. He was rolling. He leaned and carved to the right, then carved left. *Look, Ma, I can do this!* Carve right, and . . .

Uh-oh. He was speeding up. *Keep carving to control your speed!* he told himself.

He tried to carve, but the result was more of a wiggle. The wind was in his face. He was still gaining speed. The wiggle got wigglier. Under his feet, the board began to rattle. Caleb wanted to stop, but he was already going too fast for the foot drag. He knew what Zach would tell him to do . . . the glove-down slide.

At this speed? Who am I kidding? Maybe Caleb was able to do a glove-down slide when he was practicing on a gradual slope at a slow speed, but now he was going way too fast to squat that low, turn the board sideways, and use the friction of the sideways wheels and his gloved hand against the asphalt to stop. If he tried that now, there was no doubt in his mind that he'd lose his balance and go *kersplat* on the hard asphalt.

He was still picking up speed. The board's wiggle had become an all-out wobble. The wind was blowing hard enough to make his eyes tear. Blood was pounding in his ears. The skateboard's wheels were making a loud whining sound. He must have been going a hundred miles an hour.

I'm gonna die!

○

In Sarah's bedroom, Emma looked through the shelves for that book about Anne Frank. She knew it was about a Jewish girl and the Nazis in World War II. The whole issue of the Nazis was bothering Emma. It seemed to come up now every time the eSports club met. Especially today when Ms. B nearly went bonkers over the goon squad's gray shirts and Iron Crosses. It felt so strange. World War II had ended about eighty years ago. That was before any of Emma's *grandparents* had been born. Before *TV*, for Pete's sake. Things like smartphones, texting, and Instagram were at least 50 years in the future. It was a time when girls were expected to wear skirts and blouses every day. It might just as well have been the Stone Age. Also, the Allied forces had won the war. Nazi Germany and the Axis were defeated. So why, all this time later, were the Nazis still on people's minds?

Something else nagged Emma about the Axis squad. First the custom tees, now the gray shirts and the medals. Where'd the money for those things come from? Ever since Gavin's father had gotten injured, his family didn't have money to throw around. And she got the impression that was true of Crosby's family as well.

Emma found the Anne Frank book, with its maroon cover and black-and-white photo of a cheerful-looking girl with shoulder-length dark hair. Emma remembered that Sarah had read the whole book in one weekend. She'd refused to do anything except read, eat, and sleep. Emma couldn't remember her sister doing that with any other book.

Now she was going to find out why.

○

While Zach waited at the bottom of the hill for Caleb to come down, he thought back to that afternoon's eSports match. It had been tight and close, and once again the squads had been tied going into the final round. It was clear from the start that the Axis team had come prepared with a counterstrategy. As the squads went into the ninth and final round, Zach had doubts about winning. But then, partway through, Nathan went back to his old one-man lone-wolf kill-spree mode — the approach that the rest of the Allied squad had warned him wouldn't work forever.

But it worked again today. And thanks to Nathan, the Allied team eked out the win. Probably, Zach suspected, because the last thing the Axis squad expected was for Nathan to go rogue again.

A crow landed on the road and began to peck at something. Zach realized that Caleb had still not come down the hill. Zach couldn't see the top of the hill because at the bottom the road curved to the left behind the trees. But Caleb definitely should have been down by now.

Zach jogged back around the curve. At the bottom of the straightaway, he looked up the hill. There was no sign of Caleb.

Zach felt his stomach tighten and his heart begin to race. If Caleb wasn't on the road, then the only other place he could be was in the trees. Zach pictured Caleb wrapped around a tree. He imagined calling 911. He pictured an ambulance coming, and the EMTs rolling Caleb away on a stretcher. He imagined Caleb in a hospital bed wearing a neck brace, one of his arms in a cast and his leg in another cast elevated by wires.

Zach began to panic. Where was Caleb? Which of the hundreds of trees had he crashed into? He ran up the hill, looking left and right. As he passed a patch of tall grass, he heard laughing.

Caleb quietly opened the side door. He eased himself into the house and started to tiptoe down the hall to his room.

"That you, Caleb?" his mother called from the kitchen. "Dinner's ready."

"Be there in a second," Caleb called back, ducking into his room and closing the door. The sight that met him in the mirror wasn't pretty. He definitely had to get into the bathroom and clean up before his mother saw him. He silently opened his bedroom door and slid back into the hall . . . where his mother was waiting.

Her eyes widened. "What in the world?"

Caleb froze. "It's nothing, Mom."

"Nothing? Your face is covered with scratches. You're *covered* with grass stains and mud. Were you trying to sneak into the bathroom without me seeing?"

"No," Caleb lied. He stepped back and winced from the pain that shot through his knee.

"Are you limping?" Mrs. Arnett asked.

"I'm fine, Mom."

"Fine? You look like you've been in a fight. What happened?"

"I fell off a skateboard."

His mother's jaw dropped. "Since when do you skateboard?"

"Well, I—"

"Were you wearing a helmet? Did you hit your head?"

"I was wearing a helmet," Caleb assured her. "I didn't hit my head. I just need to get into the bathroom." He took a step and winced in pain.

"You're definitely limping," Mrs. Arnett said. "I want to see that knee."

"It's okay, Mom," Caleb said. "Just give me a cold pack and it'll—"

"How do you know it isn't sprained?" she asked. "How do you know you didn't tear a ligament? You probably need an MRI. I'm calling Dr.—"

"*Mom!*" Caleb didn't know where the shout came from. Well, it came from him, obviously. But from *where* in him?

His mother froze. Caleb was sure they were both thinking the same thing. Had he ever shouted at her before?

"I think I'd know if I tore a ligament," Caleb said calmly. "Just give me a cold pack, okay? That's all I need."

His mother went back to the kitchen and got one of the cold packs they kept in the freezer in case of emergency. Caleb took it and then limped into the bathroom.

Half an hour ago he'd been on a skateboard going way too

fast. The road curved to the left, but he'd gone straight . . . into a patch of tall grass and shrubs. And he actually had tucked and rolled! Maybe not on purpose. But he'd definitely rolled before landing on his back in some wet grass. He was breathing hard. His heart was pounding. His right knee throbbed painfully, and he could feel the dampness from the recent rain seeping through his clothes. But as he stared up at some white clouds in the blue sky, he felt something else. Pride. He'd tried something new and scary, and it had been fun. And the craziest thing of all? Even though he lost control and fell, it felt great.

In the bathroom, Caleb sat down on the edge of the bathtub and pressed the cold pack against his knee. Just then his phone buzzed. It was a text . . . from Brooke Ford! She'd gotten permission to do the story. A shiver of excitement raced through him. He was going to be on KFKN!

Thanks to Ms. B's stupid lecture about the Nazis, the Axis team missed the late bus. Gavin and Mackenzie walked home. But Crosby and Tyler lived farther away and decided to see if they could get a ride. Tyler called his mother, but she didn't pick up, so Crosby tried his aunt. Because of all the medications his mom was on, she wasn't allowed to drive, but Aunt Mary said she'd come.

"Don't say anything about gaming in front of her," Crosby told Tyler.

When Aunt Mary pulled up in her car, she stared at the boys. Crosby realized why: They were still wearing their gray shirts and Iron Cross medals. He wished they'd taken off the medals before she got there. Now he was worried that she would say something embarrassing.

The boys got in the back. As Aunt Mary drove away from the school, Crosby waited for her to make a comment about their outfits, but instead she said, "What happened to the late bus?"

"We missed it," Crosby said.

Aunt Mary looked at him in the rearview mirror and narrowed her eyes skeptically, as if she knew there had to be more to the story. Crosby braced himself for whatever totally humiliating thing she might say in front of Tyler.

But all she said was "Where are we taking you, Tyler?"

"Know where Old Oak Court is, ma'am?" Tyler asked in the polite way he saved for grown-ups.

"I think so," she said.

They rode for the next fifteen minutes in silence. In the backseat, Tyler played with his plastic German soldier. He aimed it at Crosby, who took it and aimed it at the back of his aunt's head and pretended to fire. The boys shared furtive grins. When they arrived at Old Oak Court, Tyler thanked Crosby's aunt for the ride. Aunt Mary waited until Tyler disappeared into his house. Then she turned to Crosby and said, "What are you wearing?"

"It was just for the eSports club," Crosby said.

Aunt Mary backed out of Tyler's driveway, then said, "First thing tomorrow morning, I'm calling the principal."

"Don't bother," Crosby said. "Ms. B already yelled at us."

Aunt Mary shook her head in bewilderment. "I cannot believe they let you wear that in school."

Now that they were alone, Crosby felt a growing annoyance. Why did his aunt have to be what Dave called a liberal snowflake? One of those soy milk drinkers who wanted to take away everyone's guns and for whom the whole world was a trigger.

"You know, it just so happens that it's a free country," he said.

"Yes, it's a free country," Aunt Mary repeated angrily. "And that means my nephew is free to walk around dressed like a neo-Nazi white supremacist. Is that *really* what you want people to think about you?"

"I'm not a Nazi, and there's no such thing as a white supremacist," Crosby shot back, repeating something Dave had said. "I'm a patriot."

He was shocked when Aunt Mary hit the car's brakes and pulled onto the road shoulder. She glared at him, her face reddening. "Where did you hear that?"

"Nowhere," Crosby said.

"*Where did you hear that?*" Aunt Mary demanded again, this time nearly shouting. Crosby slouched in the car seat, crossed his arms, and tucked his chin into his chest.

"Let me tell you something, young man," she said. "White supremacists *do* exist. Neo-Nazis *do* exist. Racists and anti-Semites and homophobes *do* exist. And they all have something in common. They hate anyone who is different. Anyone who doesn't look like them or believe what they believe in. And you are starting to sound just like them." She pulled the car back onto the road and began driving again. "You heard that somewhere online."

"No," said Crosby.

"Then where *did* you hear it?"

"Uh, from someone in school," Crosby lied.

"Who?"

"No one you know."

"I don't have to know them," said Aunt Mary. "I just want to know who they are."

Crosby stared out the car window and didn't answer. There was no talking sense with Aunt Mary. She was a hard-core liberal feminazi who probably didn't even think men were necessary. Why else had she never gotten married? At best she was a lost cause. At worst she was the enemy.

They drove the rest of the way home without speaking. As soon as Crosby got to his room, he did the stupid homework Ms. B had assigned. According to various websites, there'd been lots of genocides in history. When Europeans settled in America, it was genocide against the Indians. Not that the Indians were ever going to do anything with the country except ride around on horses and hunt buffalos. When you thought about it, wasn't just about every war genocide? Not to mention about half the video games he'd ever played, whether he was wiping out an entire enemy or an alien race or all the dinosaurs.

○

When Zach's number popped up on Caleb's phone, he hesitated before answering. He and Zach had never spoken on the phone before. They'd always texted or talked online. For

Caleb, speaking on the phone represented a different level of familiarity. It was something he reserved for close friends. Not that Zach wasn't *becoming* a close friend. But Caleb hadn't had to decide if he was or wasn't. He knew that Zach must have been calling to see how he was after the fall. Caleb appreciated the fact that he cared. It was more evidence that Zach was a good guy.

"You okay?" Zach asked when Caleb finally answered.

"Yeah," Caleb said. "A little banged up. That's all."

"I'm really sorry," Zach said. "I shouldn't have pushed you to try that hill. You needed more practice."

"Not your fault," Caleb said. "I wanted to do it."

"Man, when I found you on your back in the grass laughing," Zach said, "I didn't know what to think."

"You looked like I'd totally lost it," Caleb said.

They shared a chuckle over the memory.

"Think you'll try again?" Zach asked hopefully.

"Sure, uh, one of these days," Caleb said. What he didn't say was that he was thinking of switching to a sport that was slightly less dangerous, like badminton.

It felt like they'd come to the end of the conversation. Then Zach said, "Well, the weekend's coming up. Want to hang out?"

Caleb detected a needy edge in Zach's voice. Here was a kid who hadn't had a lot of friends in his life. The truth was, Caleb would have been happy to do something with Zach, except that he only had Saturday, and he already had plans to meet his cousins from Springdale at the mall. Should he invite Zach along? Caleb hadn't seen his cousins in a while and was eager to catch up with them. Plus, he knew how squirrelly Zach could be around new people. Caleb was worried that it might be awkward for everyone involved.

When he said he had plans to meet his cousins at the mall and wouldn't have any other time to hang out, Zach didn't reply. Now Caleb felt bad, so he said, "But maybe we can hang out next weekend, okay?"

"Uh, yeah, sure." Zach tried to sound upbeat.

"Well, I better go," Caleb said. "See ya." He got off the phone, but the bad feeling didn't go away. Every time they got together, Zach was super nice and sincere. Why couldn't he be that way, too?

○

When Crosby found Dave online that night, he couldn't tell him about what had happened in the eSports club that day because he'd led Dave to believe that he'd graduated high school and was working in a warehouse. Before they started playing, Dave told him about a rally being planned in Franklin. Wasn't that near where Crosby lived? The event would be the following week. It was being organized by a group called Identity Evropa, who believed that America had been founded and created for white Europeans. The rally wasn't going to be against anything. It was just meant to show support for the white race. But, of course, that hadn't stopped the blue-pill snowflakes from trying to go to court to prevent it.

Dave told Crosby that his brothers needed his support, and it would be great if he could go to the rally and march with them. Crosby said he'd definitely think about it. Then he had an idea. "Know what, Dave? I'm having a problem with a bunch of blue-pill snowflakes myself. They're guys I've been gaming with forever, but now they think they're hot stuff because they're in college."

"Colleges back east, I bet," Dave said with a snicker. "So what's the problem, Croz?"

"Next time we game, I'd like to take 'em down a few notches. Got any suggestions?" Crosby said.

"Oh yeah," Dave said with a laugh. "I know just the thing."

It was nearly midnight. Emma had been reading for hours and could hardly keep her eyes open. But at the same time, she couldn't stop. She felt so much like Anne Frank. When Anne wrote that she had everything she needed in life except one true friend, Emma felt like she could have written those exact words herself. When Anne wrote about how smart her sister, Margot, was, Emma felt like she was describing *her* sister, Sarah. When Anne wrote about her resentment toward her mother for favoring Margot over her, it was *exactly* how Emma felt about her own mother.

And so, when Anne and her family had to hide in an attic from the Nazis, Emma felt like it was her and her family. She shared with Anne the confusion about why the Nazis were so determined to kill Jewish people. She felt the fear Anne felt each time the doorbell rang, terrified that it might be the Gestapo, coming to take them away.

Finally, when Emma couldn't keep her eyes open for another second, she put the book down and turned off the light. But as she lay in the dark, feeling the heaviness of sleep overtake her, she thought she finally understood what was bothering her about the eSports club.

THE WEEKEND

On Saturday, Caleb met his cousins at the mall. They shopped and ate pizza and caught up on one another's lives. After lunch they were at a kiosk trying on sunglasses when Caleb's cousin, Stephanie, nudged him and whispered, "I think we're being followed."

Caleb was trying on a pair of glasses, so he looked in the mirror to see if he could spot anyone in the background. And there was Zach, pretending to look in the window of Sephora, the cosmetics and perfume store. Caleb told his cousins he'd be right back, then went over and said hi.

"Oh, hi!" Zach acted like he was surprised to see Caleb there. He seemed as jittery and squirmy as the day two months before when Caleb came to the library to ask him to try the eSports club. Even though Caleb didn't ask, Zach offered an explanation for why he was at the mall. "A couple of months ago my uncle sent me an Under Armour shirt for my birthday, but it's too big, so I'm exchanging it."

Caleb nodded at the Sephora window. "Don't see much Under Armour in there."

Zach's face reddened. "Oh, yeah, I, uh, thought I'd get a few other things while I was here."

"Like sun-kissed body glove oil?" Caleb teased.

"Uh, for my mother," Zach quickly said, and changed the subject. "So how's it going?"

"Hanging out with my cousins," Caleb said. "I think I told you that I was going to meet them here today."

"Oh, did you?" Zach mimed slapping his forehead. "Must've forgotten. So, what're you guys up to?"

It struck Caleb that if Zach had been following them, he already knew exactly what they'd been up to. But he didn't want to embarrass him by pointing that out. In fact, Caleb was tempted to ask Zach to join them. He really was. But that wasn't what the day was about.

"Listen," Caleb said. "I'll see you in school, okay? I'm really stoked for the next match. Can't wait to hear what your strategy will be."

Zach stared down at the floor. He wasn't very good at hiding his emotions, and Caleb could see that he was disappointed. Knowing how difficult these things were for Zach, Caleb began to debate whether he should change his mind and invite Zach to join him and his cousins after all. He looked toward the sunglass kiosk to see if his cousins were still there. When he turned back, Zach was gone.

Nathan lifted the brass knocker on Tanisha Proctor's front door but didn't let it drop. *Are you ready for this?* he asked himself. *Because what happens in the next few hours is going to go a long way toward determining what your life is going to be like for the next few years.*

Nathan thought he was ready. Tanisha's UnPlug2gether was something he had prepared for. Standing in front of the bathroom mirror at home, he'd practiced thanking Tanisha for the invitation. He practiced complimenting Callie Potendo on the cool self-portrait she'd painted in art class. He planned to tell Bethany Willis that he'd seen her student council poster in the hall and was definitely going to vote for her.

And he had a strategy. He wasn't going to smile too much because he thought it made him look goofy. And if he felt himself growing nervous, he wouldn't start talking too much. *Just be cool and listen to what the other kids say. The best way to get them to like you is to act interested in them.*

Nathan let the knocker fall with a *clank!* A few moments later a woman he assumed was Tanisha's mother welcomed him inside. Since the party theme was unplugging, he put his phone in an envelope with his name on it and left it in a basket by the front door. Then he went down to the basement game room. There were about twenty kids there, playing pool, foosball, and cornhole.

Because he was new, Tanisha took him under her wing and made a spot for him at the foosball table. It had to be pure chance that the other three players at the table were Gavin, Crosby, and Mackenzie. Tyler was across the room shooting pool, which meant the whole Axis squad was there. Meanwhile, Nathan was the only one from the Allied squad.

Nathan was tense when he joined the foosball game, but Gavin was different than he was at school or in the eSports club. He appeared relaxed and actually smiled now and then. They talked about sports, and it turned out that both of their fathers were Notre Dame football fans.

As the evening continued, it seemed to Nathan that some of the Axis squad were actually warming up to him. They shared a laugh when Gavin called Ironville "the armpit of the nation." Then Mackenzie asked Nathan to be her cornhole partner, and maybe it was his imagination, but he thought she might be flirting a little. Later he wound up playing eight-ball against Tyler, who greeted Nathan by clicking his heels and extending his right arm into the air with a straightened hand. It was the salute the Germans used in World War II.

The only member of the Axis squad who wasn't friendly was Crosby. The kid was like Gavin's shadow. Whatever game Gavin played, Crosby either tried to play or stood close by watching. Nathan got the feeling that a few of the other kids had noticed Crosby's clinginess to Gavin, too. At one point, Gavin told Crosby to go upstairs to get some ice for the sodas, and the kid hopped right to it. *What a twerp.*

WEEK EIGHT

THE AXIS: 3
THE ALLIES: 4

Caleb wandered into the kitchen bleary-eyed and tired. He felt like he'd hardly slept. The photographer was more than a week late with the yearbook portraits, and Caleb was worried. Had he made a mistake by recommending the guy? The yearbook was on a tight schedule. Not only would it cost a ton of money if they had to hire another photographer to reshoot all the student portraits, but the yearbook company would charge them extra for being late.

At first, Caleb was so preoccupied with worry that he didn't notice that his father was having coffee alone at the kitchen table. Caleb went to the cupboard, imagining what it would be like if just for once he found a brand-new box of Cinnamon Toast Crunch. But the only cereals were oatmeal and the antioxidant high-fiber gluten-free cardboard-flavored variety. Caleb poured himself a bowl and doused it with almond milk.

"No green hair today?" Mr. Arnett asked.

Now Caleb noticed that his father was alone, which meant

that his mom had already left for work. That seemed odd, since his parents almost always left together.

"Not today," Caleb said, and nearly gagged on a spoonful of the cereal. Was there anything worse than soggy cardboard for breakfast?

"What's the latest with Brooke Ford?" his father asked.

"It's going to be a few weeks before she can begin working on the story," Caleb said. He felt both excited and disappointed. The good news was that not only did KFKN plan to send a video crew to the school to record the eSports club in action, but they also wanted Caleb and his parents to come to the KFKN studios to be interviewed! The bad news was that Brooke Ford had a really busy schedule, and the story would have to wait until she found time to do it.

"Have you thought about the questions she might ask?" his father said.

"Like why I thought it was a good idea to have an eSports club?" Caleb guessed.

"I'd prepare myself for more than that," his father advised. "My impression of Ms. Ford is that she likes stories with controversy. A seventh grader who fights for an eSports club may be enough for ITV. But for the story to play on KFKN, it's going to need something juicier."

"Like she'll ask if I think eSports is appropriate in schools?" Caleb asked.

"You already answered that in the ITV story," Mr. Arnett said. "But what if she asks why one team always plays the German side?"

Not that again, Caleb thought wearily. "It's just a game, Dad."

Mr. Arnett adjusted his glasses. "Being played by kids who've dressed up in uniforms reminiscent of the Nazis and who sometimes joke around in German accents."

"Come on," Caleb said. "They're just playing."

Mr. Arnett planted his elbows on the kitchen table and leaned forward. "You're aware that for the past few decades there's been an uncomfortably high level of hate speech and hate crime in this country, Caleb. And all too often they're perpetrated by people who identify with Nazis, racists, and white supremacists."

Caleb brought a spoonful of soggy cereal halfway to his lips, then stopped. It had just occurred to him that this wasn't random breakfast conversation. His father had planned it. That was why he hadn't yet left for work. But maybe it was a good thing. There were certain delicate questions you sometimes wanted to ask, but there were very few people you felt safe asking. "Dad, why should people around here care? I mean, are there any Jews in Ironville?"

Mr. Arnett took a sip of coffee. "I don't know, Caleb. And that's not the issue. The issue is that the hate symbolized by the Nazis is very much alive in this country. Not just against Jewish people, but against black people, brown people, Muslims, immigrants . . . anyone who isn't white and Christian. Honestly, son, I find it incredibly disturbing that anyone would make a game of it. And to call it *The Good War*? Have people forgotten what actually happened during World War Two? *It was the largest recorded genocide in the entire history of the human race*, Caleb. Six million Jews and millions of Slavs and Russians. Gays and people with disabilities. Somewhere between *fifteen and twenty million* human beings, Caleb. Slaughtered for no military purpose. Can you imagine the number of extermination camps the Nazis needed to kill that many?"

Caleb shook his head. He'd never thought about that.

"And this ridiculous idea that it was just the Nazis who did it?" Mr. Arnett went on. "That somehow the Wehrmacht, the everyday German soldiers, didn't know? Think about it, Caleb. The geographic area in which most of those camps existed, in which most of those people were murdered, was smaller than the state of Texas. Imagine for a moment that the state of Texas contained hundreds of concentration camps. Imagine that nearly twenty million people were executed over a period of five or six years. Do you really believe you could live in Texas and not know about it? That you wouldn't hear something from a friend or a storekeeper or a stranger? Or see something yourself? Or smell it?"

"Smell it?" Caleb repeated uncertainly.

"Millions of bodies incinerated in ovens," his father said. "The stink of death must've been everywhere."

Caleb's stomach churned. He swallowed back bile.

"Not every German was a Nazi, but nearly every German soldier had to know what the Nazis were doing," Mr. Arnett said. "So the idea that your game is somehow okay because the players are pretending to be the Wehrmacht is nothing short of ridiculous."

Mr. Arnett refilled his coffee cup. "Caleb, the people who perpetuate Nazi symbols today, and those who draw swastikas on walls and wave Confederate flags, are haters and racists. It almost doesn't matter if it's the Jewish people they hate, or black people or Muslims or Hispanics. What matters is that they are promoting hate against other human beings. What matters is that they are promoting lies and falsehoods. And in doing so, they are harming humanity as a whole."

The cereal had turned the almond milk in Caleb's bowl the grayish color of concrete. It didn't matter. He'd lost his appetite.

"Every person in this country has the same choice the German people had in World War Two," his father continued. "They can stand by and watch, feeling frightened and believing there's nothing they can do. Or they can do something."

The kitchen was still. Mr. Arnett's words echoed in Caleb's ears. He knew that his father had spent a lot of time preparing that speech. He'd probably even done research. And for his father to do that meant that it was a lot more serious than Caleb had allowed himself to admit.

○

When Caleb got to his locker that morning, Emma was waiting for him. He assumed that she wanted to discuss the strategy for that day's match, but he was wrong.

"Have you ever read *The Diary of a Young Girl?* she asked. Caleb frowned. "Why would I read a young girl's diary?"

"It's about Nazism," Emma said. "Well, it's really about this girl whose family had to hide from the Nazis during World War Two. It's really disturbing."

Caleb was about to ask what she found so disturbing when

Ms. Dean came down the hall. "Caleb, I heard from the photographer," she said. "He's going to email the portraits this afternoon. We'll go over them after school."

"I can't," Caleb said. "I've got the eSports club."

Ms. Dean frowned. "This is a lot more important than playing video games. And it can't wait. Especially if we have to schedule retakes."

"Can you get someone else to do it, and I'll join you as soon as the eSports club is over?" Caleb asked.

The bell rang. Emma headed for class, leaving Caleb with Ms. Dean, who was now glowering at him.

"I think you're showing terrible judgment, Caleb," the yearbook advisor said, then turned and marched away. Caleb's ears burned. No one had ever accused him of showing bad judgment before. Suddenly everything was becoming overwhelming. Zach, Nazis, his parents, eSports, KFKN, the yearbook . . . The pressure was coming from way too many directions.

○

Nathan held his arm out straight and pulled back on his fingertips as he strode down the hall toward the computer lab. He was getting his wrists limber. It was match day, and he was feeling great. For once, there hadn't been a peep from Emma about strategy. And he knew why. Because all the strategy they'd discussed before the previous matches had nothing to do with winning. They'd won because when the fighting got close and tight, Nathan took things into his own hands. He hadn't been a jerk about it. He'd just done what was necessary to win.

And he planned to do the exact same thing today.

Emma was in shock. Through her headphones came the steady clop of troops marching to the beat of crashing drums and cymbals, and the shouts of someone giving an impassioned speech in German. On her monitor, *The Good War* had been replaced by a cascading flood of Iron Crosses, green frogs, swastikas, the number 14, burning crosses, nooses, and a dozen other symbols Emma didn't know the names for. It felt as if a demon had taken possession of the round.

Earlier, the match had begun normally. The Allied squad quickly won the first round. Nathan had played strategically, but Emma couldn't help wondering if that would change. Then, early in the second round, the Allied players again jumped out to a lead. It almost felt like the Axis didn't know what hit them. Then everything went haywire. The crazy marching audio. The flood of weird symbols on their monitors.

"Malware," said Zach, who was sitting next to Emma.

Wha . . . ? "From where? By who?" she asked.

Zach nodded at the Axis side of the table. A few of the Axis players stared at their monitors with confused expressions. But Crosby was grinning.

Suddenly, Nathan jumped to his feet, knocking over his chair. Before anyone could react, he sprang around the table, grabbed Crosby by the shirt, yanked him up, and started to scream at him.

○

Caleb was stunned. Why had Nathan grabbed Crosby and begun shouting at him? What was going on with their computers? Gavin was sitting next to Crosby, so Caleb expected that he'd do something to protect his friend. But Gavin just sat there and watched. It seemed obvious to Caleb that if someone didn't do something fast, Crosby was going to get the stuffing kicked out of him.

Ms. B yelled, "Stop!" at the boys, but Nathan and Crosby continued to scuffle. It felt as if everyone was waiting for Gavin to act. Finally, Zach jumped up, wrapped his arms around Nathan from behind, and started to pull him away. Now Caleb felt another shock. This could have been the first time he'd ever seen Zach touch another kid at school.

A second later, Caleb was on his feet, helping Zach keep Nathan and Crosby apart.

"He hacked us!" Nathan shouted.

"How could I?" Crosby yelled back. "I was in the middle of the match."

"Why would that stop you?" Nathan demanded while Caleb and Zach held him back.

"'Cause if you knew anything about hacking, you'd know I couldn't launch a malware attack while I was playing," Crosby yelled. "I'd have to do it from another server."

Nathan twisted and squirmed, struggling to break free from

Zach and Caleb. Now Ms. B stepped between them. "That's enough," she said firmly. "Calm down or this is the end of the eSports club."

Nathan stopped struggling. Everyone caught their breath, but Zach and Caleb stayed between Nathan and Crosby just in case the fight flared up again. It felt awkward for Caleb to be standing practically shoulder to shoulder with Zach. They hadn't spoken since seeing each other at the mall over the weekend. Since then, Zach had stopped coming to the cafeteria for lunch. Caleb sensed that he was upset about what happened at the mall. And the more Caleb thought about it, the more he wondered if Zach was right. Maybe Caleb should have been more sensitive. Inviting Zach to hang out with him and his cousins wouldn't have been so hard. Caleb had hoped that after today's match he would walk home with Zach as usual and smooth things over. But now he had to go to the yearbook office to look at portraits after the match. So talking to Zach would have to wait.

Why me? Crosby thought. *It's totally unfair!* Ms. B was marching both Nathan and him down to her room. *She can't prove I did anything! Nathan's the one who started it.*

Ms. B made them sit, then gave them the old "no one ever solved anything with their fists" lecture. She warned them that if it happened again, they'd both be written up and sent to Principal Summers. She gave Nathan an assignment to write about self-control and how he could have handled the situation differently. Then she told him he could go. Crosby couldn't believe it. *Why's she letting him go and making me stay?*

Nathan left, and Ms. B focused on Crosby. "What do you know about what happened today?"

"Nothing," Crosby said.

The wrinkles around Ms. B's eyes deepened. "When Nathan accused you of hacking, you said that if he knew anything about it, he'd know that you had to do it from a separate server. So clearly you *do* know something about hacking. Or, what did you call it . . . a hardware attack?"

Now Crosby saw his mistake. "Malware," he said quietly.

"And it happened just when the Axis side was going to lose another round," Ms. B added.

Crosby bit the inside of his lip. He knew where this was leading. She was going to accuse him of having something to do with the malware attack even though *she had no real proof.*

"And I suppose it was just a coincidence that the images that appeared on the monitors included Iron Crosses and swastikas?" Ms. B said.

Crosby stared past her at a big yellow sign on the bulletin board urging students to think about what they saw and read on the internet: *Is it True? Helpful? Inspiring? Necessary? Kind?* He didn't know what Ms. B was going to do next, but he really didn't want Principal Summers to get involved. If this incident got back to his mother and Aunt Mary, they might take him off screens for good.

Crosby knew he had to come up with an excuse, so he told Ms. B that he'd met someone online who said he could help the Axis win. "When he said he could help, I thought he meant giving us a secret weapon or something. I swear I had no idea he meant a malware attack that would blow up the whole match."

Ms. B's face was expressionless. As if she was trying to decide whether to believe him or not. Crosby felt himself growing more anxious. "I mean, every gamer knows what malware is," Crosby went on. "But I had no idea that was what the guy planned to do."

Ms. B still didn't react. Crosby began to feel desperate. If this got back to his mom and Aunt Mary, he was toast. It was time for the last resort—waterworks. He sniffed and wiped the tears away and swore again that he'd truly had no idea the attack was coming.

Ms. B's face softened. She pulled a tissue from a box and handed it to him. The tears had done the trick. Crosby had used them before to get out of tight situations. The great thing about tears with teachers was that you knew the story wouldn't get out. He didn't have to worry about anyone else learning that he cried.

Of course, Ms. B couldn't let him go without a lecture about the dangers of the internet and how he had to be super careful when it came to who he communicated with. And of course, Crosby pretended to agree with everything she said. He figured the final step would be some stupid assignment like the one she'd given Nathan. But instead she stood up and said she had to get back to the computer lab.

And just like that, Crosby was free to go.

Except for the incessant tapping of Zach's feet, it was quiet in the computer lab. Caleb had gone to a yearbook meeting. Gavin, Mackenzie, and Tyler sat with their arms crossed. Emma glanced toward Zach. He'd turned his chair away and pulled his hoodie down over his forehead so that his face was mostly hidden. His knees were pumping like pistons. Each time Emma replayed in her head what had happened, she thought of how Zach had been the first to try to break up the fight. This was a kid who'd been picked on for years and never fought back. And who had Zach protected? Crosby, the kid who'd probably picked on him more than anyone else.

Ms. B returned and gave them all a lecture. One more outburst like today's and there'd be no more eSports club. She meant it. They could go.

It was too early for the late bus, so everyone either had to hang around school and wait, or walk home. Saying she had papers to grade, Ms. B went back to her room. She warned them not to touch the computers. She wanted the district tech to check them before they were used again.

The Axis squad left, but Zach stayed behind. Emma did, too. Zach wasn't sure what he was waiting for. Was he hoping that Caleb would come back from the yearbook office so they could walk home together? For Zach, hanging out and skateboarding with Caleb after the eSports club had become the highlight of each week.

But then the thing at the mall happened, and Zach began

to have doubts. Why hadn't Caleb invited him to hang out with his cousins? Part of Zach's brain said that it proved that Caleb wasn't a real friend. But another part said that of course Caleb would want to be with his cousins. Especially since he didn't see them that often. Zach knew that deep down he really did want Caleb to be his friend. But there'd been kids in the past who'd only pretended. And nothing was worse than that. Given a choice between a fake friend and no friend, he'd learned the hard way that it was best to have none.

"Zach?" Emma's voice brought him back from his thoughts. He raised his head, surprised that she'd spoken to him.

"Any idea how that hack happened?" she asked.

It was a good question. Zach was familiar with the typical hacks and spam, like some griefer's lame attempts to troll a chat, or some joker using basic user script to flood screens with offensive messages. But he'd never seen image spam before.

"Not sure," Zach said. "I'll have to research it."

Just as he said that, Nathan came in. "Research what?" he asked, fetching his backpack.

"How that malware attack happened," Emma said.

"What difference does it make?" Nathan asked. "They were being jerks. I say next match we hack 'em right back. Go for the jugular. Spawn kill 'em."

Emma wasn't surprised by Nathan's knee-jerk response. Someone hits you, you hit them. Maybe in the end you'd win the fight. Maybe you wouldn't. But either way, you were bound to suffer cuts and bruises. "And then they hack us again. And pretty soon it's not a game anymore, it's just an all-out hack-athon."

"Oh yeah? So, what do *you* suggest?" Nathan challenged her.

Zach wondered why Nathan always acted like such an aggro jerk. He wondered if Emma was thinking the same thing. There was a lot to think about. Not just how the malware had been launched, but about all the hate symbols. Why *those* images? Who had chosen them?

Zach was so lost in thought that he didn't realize Nathan was speaking to him. "And what about *you*, Mr. Squad Tactician? You're supposed to be the gaming expert around here. What do *you* think we should do?"

Blinking fast and making snorting sounds, Zach reached for his backpack and skateboard. Emma was sure he was going to bolt. Should she speak up and defend him? Before she had time to decide, Zach stood . . . and faced Nathan. He was stock-still. Suddenly not a twitch or a snort. Nathan blinked with surprise as if that was the last thing he expected. Then, in a measured voice, Zach said, "I think we should let them hack us all they want."

Again, there was quiet in the computer lab. Emma was struck, not just by what Zach had said but by the way he'd said it. Self-assured and without any of the usual jitters or goofiness.

"That's the stupidest thing I ever heard," Nathan argued. "What's the point?"

But Emma saw the point. It wasn't stupid. It was smart and insightful. "He's right," she said. "What's the point of having a club if all you're going to do is cheat?"

Nathan's face grew pinched. Emma could tell that he

knew Zach was right. Not that Nathan would ever admit it. Instead, he spun around and headed out the door without saying goodbye.

Now Zach and Emma were alone in the computer lab. Outside, the sun was shining, and Emma decided she wouldn't mind walking home after all. When she stood up, Zach gave her a curious look. It struck Emma that in all the weeks they'd been together on the Allied squad, they'd never had a chance to talk one-on-one.

"Feel like walking?" she asked.

Zach started to do his rapid-blinking thing, then caught himself. "Uh, okay, sure."

They left the lab. School might have been over, but the building wasn't empty. Out of nowhere four DIY model cars came racing toward them. Emma and Zach jumped out of the way as the little cars zipped past, their electric motors whining. The cars turned at a small orange traffic cone down the hall. One took the turn too quickly and rolled over, but the other three raced back past Emma and Zach before skidding around a corner and disappearing.

"Radio controlled," Zach said. "With minicams."

Keeping an eye out for more small high-speed vehicles, they walked toward the school lobby. Once again Zach began clearing his throat and sucking air noisily through his teeth. Hoping to help him relax, Emma said, "That was really smart, telling Nathan we shouldn't do anything about the malware attack."

Zach didn't reply. Suddenly he stopped. He was staring off, lost in thought. "I have to go back," he said, and jogged away up the hall.

When Caleb got to the yearbook office, Ms. Dean and Callie Potendo were huddled together in front of a computer screen, looking at the student portraits the photographer had sent. Callie was one of the yearbook's staff writers, but Ms. Dean must have corralled her for the job of reviewing the portraits.

"Okay, I'm here," Caleb announced. He expected Ms. Dean to give him a chilly reception and for Callie to be glad to be relieved of the drudgery. Both of them looked at him.

And smiled!

"Caleb, they're wonderful!" Ms. Dean gushed. "The lighting, the expressions, the cropping . . . They're fabulous!"

Caleb was caught completely off guard. "Any retakes needed?"

"Maybe two or three," Callie said. "But that's all. And we're almost finished."

"You don't have to stay," Ms. Dean said. "We'll be done in a few minutes."

Caleb left the yearbook office feeling befuddled. It sounded like he didn't have to worry about being accused of showing bad judgment after all. The photographer he'd chosen might have been disorganized, but according to Ms. Dean and Callie, the portraits were great. Caleb wondered if there still might be time to catch up to Zach and walk home with him, but he had one more stop to make—Ms. B's room. After the malware incident today, he was worried that she might be having second thoughts about the eSports club. He'd invested so much time and energy to get it going. And now, with the Brooke Ford interview on the horizon, he was determined to keep it going.

When he got to Ms. B's room, she was sitting at her desk, grading papers. Ms. B looked up and waved him in.

"Don't worry," she said, as if she could read his mind. "I'm not going to shut down the club."

Caleb felt a weight lift from his shoulders.

"But I have to tell you," Ms. B went on, "that I am extremely disturbed by what happened. I thought we could stop it by banning the uniforms and Iron Crosses. But after today, it no longer feels like a game. It feels like what was supposed to be pretend evil has seeped into the real world."

Caleb didn't try to argue. He said that he thought the solution might be exactly what she'd said earlier: talking things out.

"Would you start by giving Nathan a call tonight?" Ms. B suggested. "To smooth things over?"

Caleb wasn't thrilled by that idea. There wasn't only tension between Nathan and Crosby. There was tension between Nathan and the rest of the Allied squad as well. The classroom got quiet. Ms. B tapped her pencil against the desk and glanced down at the papers she'd been grading. Caleb sensed that they'd reached an "Is there anything else we need to talk about?" moment. But before he left, he had one more thing to say: "I know things aren't going the way we hoped. But it's the beta test, right? There are always gonna be a few bumps in the road when you try something new."

A thin smile worked its way onto Ms. B's lips. "You're right. Thanks for reminding me. And it isn't all bad news. What did you think of Zach today? Being the first one to break up the fight?"

"Pretty amazing," Caleb said.

Ms. B's smile grew. "I know it's a cliché to say someone's come out of their shell but I can't thank you enough for what you've done. He really has become a new person."

She was right. And that made Caleb feel even worse about how he'd treated Zach at the mall. It was selfish and unkind. He just hoped he could still make up for it.

Heading toward the computer lab, Zach thought about the RC cars that had come racing unexpectedly up the hall. Just like the malware attack had come unexpectedly. And how did you stop a hacker? The same way you stopped those cars. By building a wall. For the malware, the wall meant some kind of two-factor authentication. They already had passwords, so all the club had to do was activate a second level of sign-in, like a text confirmation to each player's phone. Anyone who didn't send back the confirmation wouldn't be able to sign in and play. It was so simple that he couldn't believe he hadn't thought of it sooner.

Zach had just reached the computer lab when he remembered that Ms. B had insisted that no one touch the Providias. But he wanted to share his idea with her so he continued past the lab and headed up the hall to her room. He was just about to knock on her door when he saw Caleb inside. "If you look at where he was only a few months ago," Ms. B was saying, "lost, constantly clowning and misbehaving, never making eye contact, barely performing academically . . . and where he is now."

Zach stiffened. *She's talking about me!*

"I think back to the day I asked you to get him to join the club," Ms. B continued. "*You* saved him, Caleb."

"Well, I . . . I don't know." Caleb bowed his head. The truth was, in some ways it felt like the opposite. Getting to know Zach had saved *him*.

"But you did!" Ms. B insisted. "If you could hear what the other teachers are saying about him now. What an extraordinary transformation it's been. I'd really like to tell them about your part in it. I know they'd be grateful, Caleb. And you deserve so much of the credit."

Never one to turn down credit, Caleb said, "Well, if you insist."

Out in the hall, Zach staggered back from the door, feeling like he'd been shot with a Mega-Blaster. Of course Caleb hadn't wanted to hang out with him at the mall! He'd never truly wanted to be Zach's friend. All Zach had been to him was one more opportunity for extra credit.

Zach backed away, turned, and began to sprint. Down the hall, through the lobby, and out of school. Running as hard as he could.

WEEK NINE

THE AXIS: 3
THE ALLIES: 4

When the first bell rang, Zach was in his usual hiding place in the boys' room. He let himself out of the stall and paused to look at the ceiling. The mystery of the hanging loogies still intrigued him. *How did Gavin do it?*

Just then, the boys' room door opened. *Speak of the devil!* It was Gavin. Zach froze. The big red-haired boy stopped when he saw what Zach was looking at.

Without a word, Gavin cleared his throat, tilted his head back, and fired. A moist brownish loogie smacked into the ceiling. From its center it started to droop. The two boys watched in suspense. Would this loogie's adhesive mucus properties be strong enough? Would it dry into a perfect, elongated, teardrop-shaped stalactiloogie?

The central bulb of loogie slowly sagged. It seemed like only a matter of seconds before the force of gravity would overpower the stickiness unique to Gavin's phlegm. But then, just when it looked like the ever-thinning ligament between ceiling and mucus bulb could no longer bear the weight . . . it stopped! Zach stared up in awe. Gavin had produced a perfect three-inch-hanging loogie! Had mucus ever created anything so magnificent before?

Despite the frightening prospect of being so close to the enemy, Zach couldn't help but nod appreciatively. *Bravo, Gavin. You have proven to be without equal in the dark art of loogie launching. You are the True Hanging Loogie Master.*

But then Zach braced himself. The magical moment of the perfect stalactiloogie had passed. It was just him and Gavin, alone in the boys' room.

When Gavin pulled something out of his pocket and tossed it, Zach flinched, assuming whatever Gavin was throwing at him was bad. But it was small and looked harmless. Zach caught it: a piece of caramel wrapped in cellophane.

With the slightest smile, Gavin said, "The secret ingredient."

The Franklin bus station was a dozen blocks from the square where the rally would take place. Crosby felt tormented by nervousness and regret. He'd never skipped school before. What would his mom do when the attendance office called and asked where he was?

And here he was in this city all by himself. Even the shorter buildings in Franklin were taller than any in Ironville. And there were hardly any trees or grass. Just streets and sidewalks. And stoplights at every intersection. A block away, Crosby could see a crowd of men, many dressed in tan slacks and white or colorful Hawaiian shirts. Some were wearing black helmets and sunglasses or goggles. Others had masked their faces with bandannas. They were carrying shields and white flags with black crosses.

Crosby caught his breath and trembled. He was scared. This wasn't a video game. Those weren't avatars on a screen. They were real grown-ups—and many of them were big. Some carried metal rods or clubs. Crosby had walked about six blocks from the bus station, but now he seriously contemplated turning back and taking a bus home.

But the men with the shields and flags were just marching. It didn't look like they were causing trouble. Besides, Crosby knew it was too late to undo what he'd already done. The next bus to Ironville wouldn't leave until noon. By the time he got back, school would be over, and his mother would have been called by the attendance office. He was in big trouble no matter what.

Crosby decided to follow the marching men from a safe distance. He wanted to see what they would do.

○

As Nathan walked toward the cafeteria for lunch, he couldn't have been happier. Well, that wasn't true. If he were still back in his old town and going to his old school with his old friends, he was sure he would have been happier. But if he had to be here in stupid Ironville, things had definitely gone from bad to better. That past weekend he'd gone bowling with Bethany Willis and some of the other popular kids. He felt like he'd passed the test and had been welcomed into their crowd. In fact, he decided that this was the day he'd switch lunch tables and sit with Bethany and Tanisha.

When Nathan stepped into the cafeteria, he stopped short. For a moment he couldn't believe what he was seeing. Could that really be Zach sitting at Gavin's table? No way. It wasn't possible.

But it was. Nathan headed toward the table where Caleb and Emma sat. They were also staring at Gavin's table as if they too had just noticed.

"No, you're not seeing things," Emma said when Nathan joined them.

"If he's sitting with them, does that mean he's switched to the Axis side?" Nathan asked.

"That's what we're wondering," Emma said.

"No one's asked him?" said Nathan.

Emma started to get up. "I think the time has come."

Nathan had to admit that he was impressed. The mousy Emma he'd met a few months ago when the eSports club began would never have marched over to Gavin's table. Now he followed her and Caleb. When Zach saw them, he stared down at his lunch, averting his eyes. But the big grin on Tyler's face said it all. Zach had gone over to the dark side.

Before any of them had a chance to ask why, Makenzie said, "There's no rule that says gamers can't switch sides."

"Whose place is he taking?" Caleb asked.

"Crosby's not here today," said Tyler.

"Last week it was the malware attack," Emma said. "This week you're stealing our players. It's like, if you can't win fair and square, you'll bend the rules until you find a way. What's the point?"

It was Gavin who answered: "Chill, Emma. It's just a game."

"Only, now we're short a player," Nathan said.

"There must be a hundred kids who're dying to play," Tyler said. "It won't be hard to find someone."

Caleb cared less about the match and more about why Zach had switched sides. "Was this your decision?" he asked him.

Zach looked away and didn't answer. Nathan felt disgusted. This proved what he'd always known: that Zach was basically spineless. Like an amoeba that changed shape to fit into whatever place it found itself. Nathan didn't know what the Axis squad had done to get Zach to switch sides, and he decided he didn't care. In fact, he was happy about it. Tyler was right that it probably wouldn't be hard to find someone to take Zach's place. And then, this afternoon, without their vaunted squad tactician, the Allies would once again thrash the Axis. And when that happened, it would be clear once and for all that it was because of Nathan's superior gaming skills. Not because of Zach's so-called strategies.

"I told you Zach was a jerk," Nathan said as he, Emma, and Caleb walked away from the Axis table. Caleb knew that wasn't true. There was a big difference between someone who sometimes acted weird—because they were insecure—and someone who was a jerk. In fact, if anyone on their squad had proved themselves to be a jerk, it was Nathan.

But Caleb still couldn't understand why Zach had switched

sides. He'd been a valued member of the Allied squad. It was the *last* thing Caleb ever imagined Zach doing. Deep down, Caleb had a feeling that Zach had done it because of him. Was their friendship over? Would they never walk home together again? To be honest, it hurt.

They were halfway back to their table when Nathan veered off, saying he was going to sit with Tanisha and Bethany. Caleb got the feeling that Nathan wasn't just going to Tanisha's table for the day. It was a permanent move.

The period ended. Even though Zach sat with the Axis squad at lunch, he didn't leave with them. Caleb went into the hall and waited. When Zach came out of the cafeteria and saw Caleb, he hesitated for a moment but didn't stop. Instead, he lowered his head and quickened his pace. In a way, Caleb felt proud of him. There had been a time when Zach would have sensed trouble and immediately run in some other direction to avoid it. Even if it meant taking the long way through the corridors and being late for class.

A moment later they were walking together. *How do you start a conversation when you both know exactly what you're going to say?* Caleb wondered. So he simply asked, "Why?"

"You know why," Zach answered.

"Honestly, Zach. If I knew, I wouldn't have asked."

"You're not my friend," Zach said. "You never were. You only acted friendly because Ms. B told you to. All this time, you were sucking up to her. Just for more extra credit."

Caleb winced. It felt like Zach had stabbed him with a knife. "Okay, maybe that *was* true . . . for like, a minute. But that day we hung out in the library and you showed me the biggest wave ever surfed? I could tell that you were a pretty cool guy. And then at the informational meeting? Yeah, it was obvious you weren't going to join the club because of that jerk, Crosby. And yes, Ms. B did ask me to get you to change your mind. But know what? I would have done it anyway. Because it ticked me off. You'd already said you liked *The Good War*, so why shouldn't you join? When I walked home with you, it was because *I wanted* to get you to change your mind. Here's the thing, Zach. I like hanging out with you. You're cool, and it's the one afternoon a week that I don't have to rush to some stupid after-school activity. It's like freedom for me."

Zach smirked. "I have to hand it to you, Caleb. You are good. *Really* good. Everything you say sounds so real. So sincere. I bet I would have believed every word of it . . . if it wasn't for what happened last week after the malware attack. See, I was leaving school with Emma when it hit me how to block that hacker. The whole two-part authentication thing. But when I went to Ms. B's room to tell her, you were there. And I heard everything she said, Caleb."

Caleb racked his brain to remember what he and Ms. B had talked about that could have turned Zach against him. He didn't have to wonder for long.

"You did such a good job of getting me to join the club that Ms. B wanted to tell all the other teachers," Zach said. "She wanted you to get the credit. And you were glad to accept it."

Caleb cringed. "That has nothing to do with us being friends, Zach. I swear."

Instead of answering, Zach started to walk faster. Caleb quickly caught up. "Does this have something to do with what happened at the mall?"

"You've never wanted to be seen with me outside of school,"

Zach said. "You've never once invited me to your house. Or to do anything with you and your other friends."

So there's the answer, Caleb thought. It wasn't just that he hadn't invited Zach to hang out with him and his cousins at the mall. It wasn't just that Zach had overheard what Ms. B had said to him in her room after the malware attack. It was those two incidents *plus* what Zach had just said about Caleb never wanting to be seen with him. Caleb could have told Zach that he never asked friends over to his house because he wanted to spare them the scrutiny of his overbearing parents. But he suspected that Zach's mind was made up.

"I still don't get how you could go over to Gavin's squad," Caleb said.

"Simple," said Zach. "He asked me to. Maybe you don't really know Gavin. Maybe you assume that because he's big and a football player he has to be dumb. You think he'd have to be a jerk to want to be friends with someone like Crosby. But what if I told you that Gavin was the one who told Ms. B about Crosby's plan to cheat on that geometry test?"

Caleb stopped short. *Gavin?* For a moment it sounded absurd. But then slowly it began to make sense. Gavin was the only other person who knew about the scheme. *But why would Gavin do that?*

Crosby followed for several blocks while the men with the clubs and shields marched. Up ahead, the column was turning a corner. Walking behind them, Crosby couldn't see what was around the corner. But the men began to chant loudly: "You will not replace us!" and "White lives matter!"

Getting closer, Crosby heard angry shouting in response to the chants. Again, he hesitated and thought about turning back to the bus station. But it was just shouting, and he wanted to see what it was about. He reached the corner. The chanting and shouting were louder and fiercer now. It sounded like a confrontation, but from his spot at the back of the marchers, Crosby still couldn't see. Suddenly a soda can plummeted out of the sky and clunked heavily against the asphalt near him. Crosby bent to pick it up. It weighed far more than a soda can should have, and he quickly discovered why. It was filled with cement.

The shouting continued. At the back of the crowd, Crosby jumped up and down, trying to see what was happening. He caught glimpses of a different crowd facing the marchers. It was made up of men and women carrying signs that said "Black Lives Matter," "Love All," and "Against Hate."

As the groups hurled angry insults at each other, Crosby felt the air quiver with rage and tension. Another soda can sailed out of the sky and thudded against the street. A man wearing a black bicycle helmet and carrying a Confederate flag picked it up and hurled it back. Now both crowds were throwing cans at each other. The ruckus grew louder, and from the front came the grunting and scraping of physical confrontations. Crosby jumped up, again trying to see. It looked like the two crowds were clashing, swinging fists and clubs.

Fear overtook him. Never in Crosby's life had he been this close to such mayhem and violence. Everyone was bigger than him. Everything seemed out of control. Two men staggered toward him, helping a third whose head and white shirt were red with blood. It was like war; *real* war. Crosby had seen enough. He turned to leave, but the street behind him was suddenly filled with commandos dressed in black, and carrying shields and wielding long black rods. Like an invading army in a video game, their faces were hidden behind dark visors. Then Crosby saw the large white patches on their chests that said POLICE.

He was trapped. Behind him was the wall of approaching police commandos. Ahead, the mob of clashing marchers was slowly backing toward him. People were still shouting, screaming, swinging clubs at each other. Cans and bottles were flying and crashing to the ground. Some hit people near him. Others thudded against shields. Crosby swiveled his head this way and that, desperately searching for an escape route. Suddenly someone backed into him, knocking him to the ground. A man with a beard tripped over him, and Crosby was slammed to the asphalt. His heart beating wildly, terrified of being trampled, Crosby started to push himself to his feet.

But now his eyes and lungs began to burn. He couldn't breathe. It felt as if the air was filled with invisible, noxious fumes. His eyes were tearing so badly that he could barely see. From all around him came the sounds of brawling. Crosby panicked. Gasping for air, blinded, and terrified, he held his hands out, staggering toward what he desperately hoped was safety.

Emma was in the hall when she saw Gavin and Tyler at Tyler's locker. There had been a time not too long ago when the last thing she would have done was confront them. But that was then.

Nearing them, Emma heard Gavin say something about Franklin and seeing Robbie again. But when he saw Emma, he stopped talking. The old nervousness welled up inside her, but she kept going. She could feel her pulse racing as she stopped in front of Gavin. "Have you tried that new FIFA game?" she asked.

The slightest tic fired under Gavin's left eye. An amused smile formed on his lips. "You want to change games now that Zach's on our side? We didn't ask to change games when you were wrecking us."

"It's not about winning or losing," Emma said. "It's about finding a game that doesn't cause so many problems."

"You're just freaked because you got hacked last week," Tyler taunted.

"It's not that," Emma said.

"Then what is it, Emma?" Gavin asked. "We're not wearing the shirts or medals anymore."

Tyler clicked his heels and extended his right arm into the air with a straightened hand. "Jawohl, Herr Kapitan! But vee vill still fight on like good Germans!"

Emma was stunned. After everything that had happened, Tyler was *still* joking around? The sight of him doing the Nazi salute in the school hallway completely threw her. She looked around to see if anyone else had noticed, but if anyone had, they weren't reacting the way she was. "Do you have any idea what you just did?" she asked.

"Yeah, the German army salute," Tyler said.

"The *Nazi* salute," Emma stressed.

Tyler shrugged. "Same difference." The bell rang. He slammed his locker door shut. "See you at the match, Emma. If your squad doesn't chicken out."

He strode off. Emma was still in shock. Tyler had just done the Nazi salute in the middle of the hallway as if it didn't mean anything. As if it weren't a reminder of the millions of people who'd been slaughtered in World War II. As if it didn't symbolize hate and racism.

"Idiot," Gavin muttered under his breath.

Emma looked at him, astonished. "Sorry?"

"You heard me," Gavin said. "I swear, Emma, I can't wait to get out of here and never see any of these jerks again."

Emma was baffled. "I . . . I thought they were your friends."

Gavin snorted. "Not in a million years. Just a bunch of leeches. But as of Saturday, they're history."

"Why?"

Gavin's forehead bunched. "Your parents didn't tell you? We're moving so my dad will be closer to physical therapy. And I'll get to play on the Franklin team with Robbie."

Emma must have still looked shocked because Gavin scowled and said, "What?"

"I . . . I'm just surprised," Emma said. "I thought you liked your squad."

Gavin slowly shook his head. "After Robbie moved I probably should have made more of an effort to make new friends. But I knew we were trying to move, too, so I figured why bother? That's when the leeches started to latch on."

It had been a long time since Emma and Gavin had said

more than a handful of words to each other. She'd assumed he liked being with people like Tyler and Crosby.

"Can I ask you something, Emma?" Gavin said. "How come you've been so unfriendly to me?"

School was over, and it was time for the eSports club. Last week's match had been interrupted by the malware attack, so the semester score was still the Allies: 4 and the Axis: 3. The computer tech had run a deep scan and removed the malware so the Providias were ready to be used again. Nathan found a kid who played a lot of TGW and would fill in for Zach, but as Caleb trudged down the hall to the computer lab, he didn't feel much like playing.

The fact that the Allies wouldn't have Zach on their side was the least of it, although Caleb doubted they'd have much of a chance against the Axis without him. Caleb tried to remind himself that it was just a game, but it really hurt that Zach had deserted their squad because of him.

As he passed the boys' room, Caleb saw something odd. The door was wide open, and Principal Summers was standing inside with a crestfallen expression on her face. It looked like she was close to tears. A custodian was using dark green paint to cover something reddish-orange on the wall. Whatever it was looked like it had been spray-painted, but most of it was now hidden under the new coat of green. Caleb couldn't be sure what had been there, but he was certain that he'd seen that yam-colored shade of spray paint before.

When Principal Summers saw him looking in from the hall, her face revealed what Caleb thought was great sadness and frustration. He was surprised. In his experience, the only two emotions she displayed were sternness and pleasure. But now she looked truly shaken. Whatever had been drawn on that wall must have really rattled her.

Caleb continued down the hall. When he turned the corner, he saw Emma and Zach outside the computer lab, looking at a handwritten sign taped to the door: ESPORTS CLUB CANCELED.

"What's going on?" Caleb asked.

Emma made a nervous fluttering gesture with her hands. "Uh, I don't know."

Zach looked away and didn't say anything.

"Well, I just saw something really weird," Caleb said, and began to tell them about the boys' room. Before he could finish, Ms. B came down the hall, looking grim. "In case you're wondering, someone drew a hate symbol on the boys' room wall," she said, sounding angry and disheartened. "Don't ask what it was. But Principal Summers and I have decided to cancel the eSports club today."

Hate symbol? Caleb was astonished. He had to force himself not to stare at Emma. Instead, he asked Ms. B, "What makes you think the two things are related?"

"If you'd seen what was drawn, you wouldn't need to ask," Ms. B said.

It's that bad, Caleb thought, again resisting the urge to look at Emma. *But it makes no sense.* "Where's the Axis team?" he asked.

"I told them to go home," Ms. B said. She gazed in at the

computer lab and sadly shook her head. "I never imagined it would come to this."

Caleb wished he could figure out what was going on. "So . . . what about next week?" he asked.

"I'm not sure," Ms. B said. "Why don't we wait a few days and then talk about it." She checked her watch. "I need to report this to the police. You might as well go home."

Ms. B left, but Emma, Caleb, and Zach dawdled. They'd missed the regular buses, and it was way too early for the late bus. *They drew a hate symbol in the boys' room just before the eSports match,* Caleb thought. He didn't know why, but he knew who did. Only, he would have to wait until the time was right to ask.

Zach cleared his throat and made some snorting sounds. Caleb wondered why he was still hanging around. Was he waiting for Caleb to say something? Was it a sign that deep down he still wanted to be friends?

"I think I better go," Emma said. Caleb suspected that she sensed that he and Zach needed to talk. Or was there another reason why she was eager to leave? She headed around a corner. In the empty corridor, Zach glanced briefly at Caleb and then stared again at the floor.

Caleb thought back to the times he and Zach had spent together over the past couple of months. The skateboarding, the pretend game casting, the funny private moments they'd shared when Caleb felt he could be as free as he wanted. It was something he hadn't experienced much. Not when he was always so busy with school and activities. Always challenging himself. Always needing to be the best. Always—to be honest—looking for ways to get extra credit. Maybe there was nothing wrong with that, as long as you took time to have fun, too.

Zach cleared his throat again and chewed on a fingernail. Caleb thought he understood why he'd switched to the Axis side that morning. He couldn't really blame the kid. Given the way Zach had been treated all these years, who could fault him for being mistrustful?

Caleb made a decision and reached toward Zach, who flinched and took a step back, as if he was afraid Caleb wanted to hurt him. But Caleb gently placed his hand on Zach's shoulder. "Hey, want to come over to my house?" he asked.

When Crosby felt arms go around his waist and lift him off his feet, he couldn't see who was carrying him. His eyes were still burning and blurred with tears. His ears were filled with the shouts and screams of people engaged in battle, but now there was also the quick heavy breaths of whoever was carrying him. Crosby had no idea who it was, or where they were going, but he didn't resist. With each thudding footfall, the person carrying him was taking him away from the violence. And Crosby was finally able to gasp air that didn't cause his lungs to burn.

To Crosby that meant that wherever they were going had to be better than where he'd just been. Because where he'd just been was a place he never wanted to go again. Nothing he'd ever experienced came close to that much violence. That much hatred. That much terror. He would have been happy if whoever was carrying him continued all the way back to Ironville.

But the person stopped. Crosby heard a car door open. Through his tearing eyes, he saw black lettering on a white background. The next thing he knew, he was in the backseat. The door slammed. The world became a little quieter, although he could still hear snatches of the mayhem outside. New smells entered his nose. The scent of vinyl car seats and stale coffee. Crosby blinked hard and tried to peer ahead. He saw a black metal grate between the back and front seats. A thought shook him. He quickly reached for the door handle.

But there was no door handle. He was locked in.

○

Emma headed toward her locker. She'd left Caleb and Zach because she had a feeling they needed to talk in private. And because there'd been something about the way Caleb looked at her that made her uncomfortable. She also needed to think about the conversation she'd had with Gavin. She'd always thought of herself as an open-minded person. But she realized now that he was right. She'd been biased and judgmental. After being childhood playmates, she'd pulled away and shunned him because he was big and rough. Because he was a football player. Because he wasn't in a lot of smart-kid classes like she was. And because she'd assumed that someone like him would want nothing to do with her. So it came as a shock today when he told her how hurt he'd felt when he realized that she didn't want to be his friend anymore.

Emma turned a corner. The long hallway was almost empty except for one person: Mackenzie. Something felt strange, and Emma stepped back around the corner and then peeked. Down the hall, Mackenzie looked around. Then she tried a locker and then another and another. Finally, she found one that opened. She looked around again and then reached in. A moment later she quietly closed the locker and started over, trying one locker after another until she found the next one that had been left open.

So that's how she could afford those clothes and jewelry, Emma thought as she took out her phone. *And I bet she's the one who paid for those custom tees and gray shirts as well.*

A moment later, Emma had what she needed, and headed up the hall. Mackenzie must have heard her footsteps because she instantly looked in her direction and then walked toward Emma. As the two girls approached each other, Emma felt the old familiar nervousness. Could she really do what she imagined doing? She knew how simple it would be to turn around. How easy it would be to pretend she hadn't just seen what Mackenzie was up to. After all, why should Emma care? She always locked her locker.

They came closer. Mackenzie glared at Emma, as if daring her to say something. Emma felt her heart thrum and her stomach knot. She hated confrontations, and Mackenzie could be so intimidating. There was still time for Emma to turn around.

But she kept going. When she was a dozen feet from

Mackenzie, she stopped. With her hands on her hips, Mackenzie snapped, "What?"

The words Emma wanted to say were in her throat, but she wasn't sure she could get them out. Mackenzie kept glaring.

"I know what you were doing," Emma said.

"What are you talking about?" Mackenzie asked in her most disdainful voice. "I wasn't doing anything."

Despite feeling like her body was being racked by tremors of fear, Emma forced herself to speak firmly. "You were going through the lockers, looking for money."

"You're crazy," Mackenzie practically spit.

"I saw you," Emma said.

"Liar."

With a trembling hand, Emma held up her phone and played the video she'd just taken. The color left Mackenzie's face. Her eyes darted like a trapped animal desperate to escape. But finally realizing that there was no way out, she hung her head. Emma studied this girl, who had treated her so meanly and tormented her for so long. It would be so easy to show the video to a teacher or to Principal Summers. Even better, to post it online for the whole world to see, and *then* show it to Principal Summers.

But instead she said, "I'm not going to tell."

Mackenzie looked up, her eyes wide. Her mouth fell open.

"I *should* tell on you," Emma went on. "But I want to show you that people can be kind and forgiving. *You* can be kind and forgiving. There's no reason why you have to be mean. People would like you more if you weren't. Maybe you'd like yourself more, too."

Mackenzie blinked. Her eyes began to glisten.

"You have to give back everything you've taken," Emma said. "Not just today, but all the other times, too." Once again, she held up her phone. "And if I ever hear that money is missing from a locker again, then I really will show this to everyone."

And with that, Emma turned her back on the Mistress of Microaggressions, and walked away down the hall. With a smile on her face that Mackenzie couldn't see.

○

In the emergency room at Franklin Hospital, Aunt Mary held a small plastic cup of water against Crosby's eye and told him to blink. The water soothed the burning. Wearing a blue paper hospital gown, he was propped up on a narrow bed in a room lined with medical equipment.

Aunt Mary smoothed his hair. When Crosby was first brought to the emergency room, the nurses made him remove his pants and shirt because both were still full of tear gas. Someone asked him his name and address, and when Crosby told them, there were murmurs and he heard someone say, "You better get Mary."

Now his aunt was here, gently attending to him. "You came all the way from Ironville by yourself?" she asked while she rubbed his neck and arms with a cleansing wipe to remove the tear gas residue.

"I just wanted to see," Crosby said meekly. He was still trembling. Still shaken by the mayhem and brutality he'd been trapped in. He hadn't been arrested. The police officer put him in that squad car for safety and then went to look for more injured marchers. When the backseat of the car was filled with gasping, nearly blinded rioters, the officer drove them to the hospital emergency room.

"You have to stay away from them, honey," his aunt said softly. "They're haters and racists. Do you really want to be like that?"

Her soothing voice and gentle touch were enough to make Crosby break down and cry. The water from the eyewash cup spilled down his paper gown, leaving a dark stain. As he sat sobbing, feeling broken and empty, he felt his aunt's arms go around him.

"Listen," she said. "I may not be a psychologist, but it's plain as day to me that this is about your mom being so sick. With your dad not around, you must be so worried about the future." Crosby sniffed and nodded.

"You don't have to be scared," Aunt Mary whispered. "I'll always be here for you. You don't have to join some white supremacist group to feel wanted. I'll always want you."

WEEK TEN

School had just ended. The boys' room was empty.

Squad tactician Goofy Foot enters the pissorium to test the new and improved advanced caramel loogie projectile. Goofy Foot has already popped a piece of caramel into his mouth. Spit adhesiveness is increasing. The countdown begins:

Ten . . . nine . . . Saliva/mucus mixture approaching desired state of viscosity.

Eight . . . seven . . . Gathering saliva/mucus ball behind front teeth.

Six . . . five . . . Adjusting lip cannon to appropriate launch angle.

Four . . . three . . . Rolling of tongue and compression of lips initiated. Deep inhalation to follow.

Two . . . one . . . fire!

The light brown loogie rocketed out through his lips.

Upward it shot.

Zach was certain that it would soon join the other loogies hanging from the ceiling.

But then, just an inch from impact, the loogie stopped.

For an instant it hung motionless in the air.

Then it plunged back down.

Splat!

Caleb and Emma walked together toward the computer lab. Ms. B had asked the eSports club to meet for a semester wrap-up.

"I sure hope you got rid of that spray can," Caleb said in a low voice as they walked down the hall.

Emma caught her breath and felt her body tense. "I had a feeling you remembered."

"Dark coral," Caleb said. "From our underwater landscape."

Emma's insides churned. *Would he tell? Was he furious at her for doing something that ended the eSports club for the rest of the semester? Would he hate her forever?* "I had to do it," she said. "It was the only way I could make them understand what they were doing."

Caleb didn't respond. He just kept walking.

"Caleb?" she said anxiously.

"It worked," he said.

Emma exhaled with relief. Just that morning there'd been an announcement that the school would start a unit for sixth graders about internet safety. They were also planning an assembly about hate speech and hate symbols.

"I was afraid you'd be mad," Emma said.

"This is the beta test, remember?" Caleb said. "We made mistakes. We learned what to do for next semester. And . . ."

When Caleb trailed off, Emma gave him a curious look. "And what?"

Caleb smiled. "And if it wasn't for the club, I'm not sure we ever would have seen Emma Lopez stand up to people like Mackenzie Storrs and Nathan Crane."

Ms. B stood by the computer lab door and waited for the gamers. For once they wouldn't be sitting at the table with the Providias. She'd arranged eight chairs in a circle so that the kids could discuss their experiences.

Caleb and Emma were the first to arrive. The next to enter was Zach, wiping his face with a paper towel.

"Oh no, not again," Ms. B said with a gasp.

Zach grinned and winked. Instead of the hoodie, he was wearing a plaid collared shirt. Of course, since it was Zach, the shirt was wrinkled, and he'd buttoned it crookedly. Still, Ms. B felt a warm glow as she watched him join Caleb and Emma. She thought back to the first informational meeting, when he'd come late and then sat far away from the others, hidden in his hoodie. Zach truly seemed like a different boy now. That alone was enough to make her believe that the first season of the eSports club had been a success.

The members of the former Axis squad were slower to arrive. Both Crosby and Mackenzie came in looking solemn.

This puzzled Ms. B. Surely they couldn't be so gloomy just because the Allied team had won the season, could they? She wondered if something else had happened that she didn't know about.

The last person to enter was Tyler, who gave Ms. B a jaunty wave and spun a chair around so that he could sit backward. *Some kids never change*, Ms. B thought. She poked her head out into the hall, but it was empty, so she closed the door and took a seat in the circle. There were eight chairs because Gavin had moved away the previous weekend. But that still left one chair empty.

"Is Nathan coming?" she asked.

Mackenzie shook her head. "He's moved on to bigger things."

Ms. B wasn't sure what that meant, but she let it go. "Well, I asked you here today to talk about the club and what you've learned."

The response among those in the circle ranged from blank expressions to small nods.

"Okay, I'll break the ice," Ms. B said. "Overall, I think the eSports club's been a good thing. But it's also a bit like Pandora's box. Once we opened it, all sorts of unexpected things came out. Some good, some definitely not good. Clearly, it's shown us that as a school, we need to focus more on internet education. We have to do more to prepare you for what you see and hear online."

Crosby raised his hand. "Are you going to do the club again, Ms. B?"

"Yes, I think so," she said. "But what are your thoughts about how we can improve it?"

Emma suggested that instead of permanent squads for the

whole semester, they switch the members of the squads for each match "so it doesn't start to feel like us against them."

Caleb said that next time they should pick a game that wasn't based on a real war.

Since they'd been able to get the computers for free, Zach wondered if they should try writing another grant for really good gaming chairs.

Ms. B turned to Mackenzie and Crosby. "Do either of you have anything to add?"

Mackenzie shook her head and then looked at Emma. For once, she didn't sneer. Her eyes were soft, almost wistful. Emma couldn't know for certain what she was thinking, but the expression on Mackenzie's face just might have meant *Thanks*.

Crosby raised his hand next. "I don't have a suggestion, Ms. B. Just something I want to say. That okay?"

"That's fine, Crosby," Ms. B said.

Crosby turned to Zach. "I learned something. I've been picking on certain people because I've been really angry about some bad things that are happening at home. But that's no excuse. What I did was wrong. And . . . I'm sorry."

Everyone turned to see how Zach would react. He leaned forward in his chair and held out his fist for a bump. Crosby bumped it.

"Ancient history," Zach said.

○

They were at the top of the big hill again. Zach had wanted Caleb to go first, but Caleb insisted Zach go. He watched as

Zach gracefully carved down the long straightaway. When he got to the bottom, Zach stopped before the bend in the road so he could watch Caleb come down.

Caleb stood at the top of the hill with one foot on the board. A breeze ruffled his hair. He took a deep breath of fresh air. He couldn't think of anyplace he'd rather be.

Down at the bottom of the long straightaway, Zach waved. "You ready?"

Caleb smiled. He'd never been more ready.

ACKNOWLEDGMENTS

My great thanks to Beverly Horowitz, who, as publisher of Delacorte Press, gave me the opportunity to write this book. Forty years ago, when we were both starting out in the publishing world, Beverly edited *The Wave*. I am grateful that all three of us are still in print. I would also like to thank Kelsey Horton for her excellent editing on this project. In addition, numerous young people and gamers served as resources for this story, including my son, Geoff; Isaac Cooper; and Walker Friedman. Thanks, guys. I am also indebted to Aimee Aslanian, Michael Masino, and Kristina Pantginis for directing me to gamers at their schools. Finally, a hat tip to the Anti-Defamation League and the Southern Poverty Law Center for the research and information they provided. Hate is not the way forward.

ABOUT THE AUTHOR

TODD STRASSER is the award-winning author of more than 140 novels for teens and preteens. His most notable works include *The Wave*, *Give a Boy a Gun*, and *Fallout*, which are taught in classrooms around the world. He lives in New York.

TODDSTRASSER.COM